I0717796

Liddle Deaths

Morgan Christie

STILL
HOUSE
PRESS

All inquiries may be directed to:

Stillhouse Press

4400 University Drive, 3E4

Fairfax, VA 22030

www.stillhousepress.org

Stillhouse Press is an independent, student- and alumni-run nonprofit press based out of Northern Virginia and operated in collaboration with Watershed Lit: Center for Literary Engagement and Publishing Practice at George Mason University.

Library of Congress Control Number: 2023947275

ISBN-13:   978-1-945233-26-5

Jacket Design and Back Image: Christopher Kardambikis
Cover Image: Altered Diagram from "Diagrams of Full Figures" by György Doczi
Interior Design: Paul Logan IV

*For all the parents/guardians and children out there,
trying to make it work*

Part 1

The Eulogy

The potato salad was the only edible thing there. Niya twirled her fork through the stringy collards, wincing as the prongs scratched the base of the plate and wondered what the hell was going on. The least they could do was cook good food. She tried everything but the pork chops; she gave pigs up a few years back—health, wellness, and other cataloged reasons. Even though her abstinence from pork consumption seemed an unlikely topic, she worried that someone would ask her why she stopped eating it. She worried because she'd have to hesitate.

The house was musty, undoubtedly due to the grieving stragglers that visited on and off throughout the day. Niya had considered escaping to dig up a buried can of Lysol and parade it around the house to combat the stifling body odor. She imagined her mother's face if she did it, the cool and very assuming way she'd stare. Niya decided she wouldn't bother; the smell of Lysol was ridiculously obtrusive.

She neared the end of her meal and glanced across the table—her mother hadn't taken a bite. Niya studied the curve of her mother's mouth as it sat motionless, the remnants of her rich wine-red lipstick staining her lower lip.

"You have to eat," Niya said.

Her mother shot her eyes up like paper darts. It had always been her way. Niya's maturation had nothing to do with anything. She was the mother, and Niya was the child. She would never listen to her daughter. To be fair, she rarely listened to anyone. What gave someone the right to tell another cognizant adult what to do or what was best for them? Niya answered that question once and was met with the very same eyes she was being met with now. She knew when to lay off. Niya lifted her hands in a sort of complacent surrender, and she pushed the chair back.

The problem with death wasn't loss for Niya, it was grief and what came along with it. To lose someone was one thing, but to have to learn to adapt to their absence was another. In that house, grief was dirty dishes. Her father had lived in the same town for over fifty years. The accumulation of family, friends, colleagues, and local small-talkers were in abundance and so were their dishes. It seemed everyone that had ever spoken to her father had been to the house several times that week, before and after the funeral. Each time, they ate. The food was never successful in filling the empty space, but there was always so much, people ate it anyway. Niya had friends and colleagues that did the opposite during times of mourning, where even the suggestion of food was a queasy concept, but not in their house. Her mother also refused to use paper plates, *tacky*, she insisted. So for the past week, Niya spent her time eating subpar food, entertaining comers and goers, and washing their dirty dishes. The part about mourning her father seemed inconsequential, she was too preoccupied with instantly mildewed dish water and the remnants of moderately decent potato salad, tasteless collards, and inedible pig. The sink, once again, was full of dishes.

It hadn't occurred to Niya that she was wearing short sleeves. When she reached to pull them up after setting her plate down, the sensation frightened her. She brushed against her skin and for a moment thought herself a stranger. She jumped at her own touch. Her hands felt soft and pearly, likely from the dish soap, and she couldn't recall the last time they'd felt so delicate. Pounding away at laptop keys the past few years had made them hard, resilient even, so the sensation caught her completely off guard. She jerked her hand off her arm like she touched a hot thing, feeling as though something was in a place it wasn't meant to be.

Niya reached for the steel wool; she had found the sponge useless against dried scraps, so she didn't bother wasting time with the niceties of porcelain surface treatment. She hunkered down and began to scrub—the same repetitive motion she'd taken to since arriving home a day after she got the call. It was the first time she and her mother had spoken in months, not out of anger, rather having simply nothing to discuss. The time they'd spoken before was when Niya informed her mother and her father the rights to her most recent novel had been picked up by a small film production company. She'd done it. Her father, ecstatic, barely let her mother get a word in. When she finally said something, Niya retracted a bit. Her mother didn't do it on purpose, Niya knew, it was just her way.

"How they making it into a movie and the book didn't even come out yet?"

Niya felt herself exhale from the throat, loud and uncaring, not realizing she was likely on speakerphone, and the sound came off even louder than she intended it too. A strained silence lingered for what seemed an entire minute. In that time, she imagined her father nudging her mother, or maybe making the slightest of head gestures to hide the obvious mediating motion, as though Niya were there to see it. She imagined his eyes moistening from excitement and dispiritedness at a time that should have solely been about the former. She imagined him staring at her, hoping she'd do what she eventually did.

"That's good Aniya, real good," her mother whispered.

Niya heard her father smile through the phone as he jumped back into miscellaneous detail ponderings and inconsequential fact checks. It was the last time she'd heard her mother's voice until about a week ago when she told her.

"He's gone."

She said it in a comfortable way, one which suggested prediction or prolonged illness. It was not the way Niya expected to hear of her father's unexpected death. Her mother had always been glacial, but she thought that call might have been different.

Niya glanced back at her mother; she was still sitting

at the table in front of the uneaten food. As Niya lifted the final plate, slight sounds of malleable steel against porcelain, it finally occurred to her, as though the recent happenings were awoken from a deep sleep. Her mother had buried her husband earlier that day, as she did her father. Her mother wasn't being the moody churl she almost always was, defying the suggestion to eat, she was grieving.

The wake was held at a local soup kitchen, an old, unmaintained community center. Niya's father began volunteering there some five years back and would always find some mildly obnoxious way to bring it up in conversation. It was harmless, but noticeable. Niya might be catching up with him about writing, the Sixers, or some other non-food related banter, but he'd manage to sneak it in there. Something about a new brand of cracker he'd discovered that they paired with the chicken noodle or a fresh fruit donation he facilitated at a farmers' market. The soup kitchen was where he found purpose—life after retirement plays a strange game with the concept—and it was where he seemed happiest. Both Niya and her mother knew that. The fact that he wasn't a prayin' man, the other thing he'd bring up in a not-so-mild way, only solidified her mother's acceptance of the ceremony not being held at a church. She didn't budge on the burial though, utterly refusing to facilitate the *desecration and downward spiral* of his body and soul. Niya only found her mother's statement amusing because of the amount of times she'd told him to go to hell.

Service was the only real propriety her father believed in. Religion talked a good talk sometimes but lacked the conviction he desired in his results. He needed to see the change he believed in, to stick his hands in and play around with it, like he was making a thick mud pie. He found it difficult to believe in anything someone told him to believe in, especially if he was expected to believe in that thing more than he believed in himself. Niya never knew exactly how to feel about that idea, but she understood it.

People began to pack in, strangers and estranged neighbors Niya had no recollection of. The process took longer than it should have because almost everyone stopped to stare at the in-memoriam portrait blown up at the door. Niya's mother chose the photo. It was her father as a young man, leaning against his prized red '77 *Deuce and Quarter*. It was his first car, favorite car, the vehicle he and her mother went on their first date in, back in '83. The choice of photo stunned Niya. She didn't imagine her mother choosing such an easygoing, laid-back picture of him. He looked taller than he was and about as handsome as he used to be, maybe a great oak reincarnated into a less still sort of life. He smiled, but it was a subtle smile, starkly reminiscent of the way Niya remembered his cheeks slowly filling. The picture seemed more like something Niya herself would have chosen rather than her mother. That reality warmed and confused her.

Niya wrote the eulogy; she was the obvious choice. While the events of the service didn't have much structure, one of her father's old co-workers acted as the master of ceremonies for the day. He was a bit pushy, a busy personality type that would normally give Niya a headache, but she felt mute to those sorts of headaches surrounding deaths and funerals. Everything was enough to give her a piercing migraine during times like these, so she figured it was some sort of bodily resistance she had built up to not being fazed as much as she usually would be. Save her mother, Anita could piss her off anywhere, at any time. Usually, watching people scurry around would do that to her sometimes, just make her angry. She'd watch them buzz along doing much of nothing, and the perpetual motion of her eyes constantly darting with them would eventually result in something slightly painful. Niya always put the need to watch these sorts of people on her *writerly nature* chart, a pull to observe all things. Her mother simply said she was nosey, and always had been.

The man would pass the mic around from guest to guest, making sure stories remained humorous and light. Niya wished she could remember his name. She only thought about it because of the man's meticulous nature, the way he awkwardly swayed towards sections of the room that seemed more solemn than gleeful, or only played upbeat R&B and jazz tracks. He was following instructions, instructions only her father could have left him. It occurred to Niya that her father and this man had discussed their deaths, and he was following through on everything that her father wanted. They must have been close, and she didn't know—couldn't even remember—his name. She did remember him mentioning her writing though.

"Your daddy sure had sumtin' for your words, baby," the man said. "Like milk honey drainin' into your ear. He tol' me that once, I ain't never forgot it."

Niya's publications, writings, and novels, all of them, made Jacob proud. They gave him something to gloat about, which Niya wasn't a fan of, but in a life of tedious physical labor, low wages, micro and macro aggressions and oppressions, classist and racial prejudice, and a thrice-mortgaged home, she believed he deserved the opportunity to if that's what he needed. Her father was the first call she made after finding out about her Pushcart selection, the news still so fresh it smelt of snapped coconut meat, a favorite snack of Niya's that still had a way of ambushing her senses when good news arose. She told him that a story of hers would be published in that year's collection and he gasped in unmeasured glee. He laughed and popped his fist against the countertop at least four times, his fervor intertwining with her own steadily growing excitement. The best part was Niya knew he had no idea what the Pushcart was, he was just so happy for her. That was the thing about her father really, she made him happy, everything about her made him happy. There was something about that happiness that filled Niya, made the holes less crevassed. Her writing helped, so did her secret bites of bacon, but nothing filled her like his happiness could. The man not so literally yanked Niya out of her thoughts when he called her to the front to read the eulogy.

A misty drizzle of remembrance began to haze through the room as Niya stepped towards the mic and thought of his happiness no longer existing in the world. She felt off balance, like the remembrances were shallow puddles already set into the beige tiling, and instead of falling, their water drizzled upward from the floor to the ceiling. Niya stopped walking, unsure of how to maneuver the unexpected sensation, of how to get her balance back. She stood with her back to the crowd and stared down at the tiles, desperately seeking the puddles she knew had to be there.

After another ten seconds or so the man touched her arm—she had sleeves this time. Niya looked at him and wondered when he had walked over to her as she watched him smile a smile that was so different from her father's, it made her breath shake like it was almost broken.

"You don't have to do this," he whispered to her.

Niya had almost forgotten why she was going towards the front. He reached for the piece of paper and gripped the corner in a gentle way, the way Niya assumed someone should grip a eulogy. He pulled it as though it was ripping, quieting his movements, and making the exchange soundless. Niya didn't release the eulogy right away, she felt tied to it. She knew it was her responsibility, that her father would have wanted her voice swimming through the center, but there were just so many puddles.

She finally let go and turned around to expressions of pure understanding, of grief, longings for laughter, and so many sympathetic eyes. All except one pair. The pair she refused to focus on but that were more pronounced than any other. The only pair that seemed to matter. As she tiptoed back to her seat, she heard the man in the background addressing the crowd.

"I loved Jacob like a brother," he expressed behind his invisible podium. "And thought I could read his sweet Niya's eulogy."

He paused, looking down at the paper, still holding it as gently as when he took it.

"But these are her words," he looked at Niya. "And shouldn't nobody speak 'em but her. Anita and Aniya decided to publish the eulogy in Jacob's favorite local paper, so we'll read it in the paper come Wednesday. Till then, we'll just remember all that Jacob meant..."

His words turned to white noise then. He wasn't going to read it. Her father's eulogy wasn't going to be read at his funeral. Niya wanted to get up, march back to the front, stain her shoes in the uncertainty, and take back the paper with the great words she'd written so she could sing them for him. Not towards the sky—he didn't believe in a heaven. Just out amongst the memories he still lived in. Niya realized there were hundreds of people packed into that small and broken community center, and no one cared about the heat or the tedious nature of repetitive stories and not so clever anecdotes, they were just there to remember. There were three days between Saturday and Wednesday, and that was too long a time for his penned memory to go unseen. He wasn't going to read it. Niya placed her palms on the sides of her chair, hoping some momentum might be the force she needed to get up. But she couldn't. She couldn't move. So she sat. She sat in the drizzle, the drops of sweat accumulated on her forehead masking the rain falling inside on top of everyone. The puddles had to come from somewhere. As she sat in the inside rain, it wasn't the dry wetness that made her uncomfortable, or the awkward touches and sighs of endearment that followed as people began to file out; it was the pair of eyes that hadn't left her since she returned to her seat. The pair of eyes she felt for the rest of the day in its entirety. The pair of eyes she felt piercing into her back, even then, as she washed what she hoped was the last load of dishes that night. It had always been her mother's way, but today, Niya feared, it was warranted. He didn't read the eulogy.

The eulogy went unread.

Niya heard her mother shift the fork on the table. A warning. She knew her mother still hadn't eaten so the necessity of the fork was solely to let her daughter know what was coming. Throat clearing of sorts. Niya's instinct was to look away, to keep her back to the inevitable firestorm. Her mother's shifting continued, as did Niya's pretending not to hear it, until finally, the fork stopped, and her mother began.

"You just ain't worth shit," her mother more so grunted than said. "You had one job. You're a writer, ain't you? Guess that doesn't make you a reader too."

"Mom," Niya glanced back at her. "Can we not. Not today, please."

"So when?" she replied. "The next time your father has a funeral?"

Niya exhaled as she dried her hands on one of the knit hand towels her mother made. It was starchy and brushed against her skin like dull sandpaper. Niya couldn't imagine her mother knitting anything other than exactly that texture. There was a brashness to everything about her, so why would she pick a soft yarn? She remembered a time when she was eight, a slapping storm hit and shook every window in the house. Niya ran to her parents' room and made her way between them. She snuggled beneath a woolly throw her mother made not even a month earlier and felt her skin scar and scrape as the blanket pulled over her skin. Niya remembered yelping and startling her mother out of her sleep.

"The blanket hurts," Niya's young fear exclaimed.

Her mother glared at her in a half daze, "Maybe it'll teach you to stay where you belong."

Niya sank into the painfully itchy sheets and wondered exactly where that place was. Two decades later, Niya found herself wondering the same thing; because she was sure she didn't belong there in that kitchen, with the tapping fork and blistering stare, either.

"I'm going upstairs," Niya mumbled under her breath.

She inched towards the stairs as her mother said, "Clean out that third room while you're up there."

Niya felt her face morph into a frown, one born of confusion. She had no idea what her mother was talking about, but she didn't inquire. She climbed the stairs she'd climbed so many times the last few days, and instead of going straight to her cell of a room, she turned before she reached the hallway's midpoint. Niya hadn't paid attention to that door in what felt like decades, even before she left for college. It always felt like a linen closet to her, being so close to the bathroom. The door leaned a little too, crooked with its faux cedar and starkly tarnished brass knob. It was a room she rarely remembered entering as a child, maybe helping to fix it up when company came and listening to her mother complain about her father's bed-making ineptitude, which she wasn't wrong about— he couldn't make a bed to save his life. A life that no longer required saving, Niya thought to herself as she pushed open the door.

She almost expected a wave of dust to rush over her as the still air from what she imagined would be a stale room crept up her nose. There was no such staleness; it smelt like the rest of the house did. Her eyes met with the pitch black as she took a step forward. For an instant, Niya couldn't remember where the light switch was. The lights were almost always on when she'd entered the room as a kid.

When she was younger, the few times she'd venture in, she always smelt fresh linen. The lingering odor would take over as her mother made up the bed for some distant relative's impending visit. The soft blue sheets would almost float mid-air in the room as her mother threw them open, and it would look like the sky had found its way inside. Once, Niya jumped on the bed under the raised sheet as her mother held the corners and spread the bedding. She knew she was going to be yelled at; jumping on the bed, creasing the sheet, and the overall free-spirited nature of the act was yell worthy. Niya waited for the screaming to begin as the sheet fell on top of her head, leaving her standing in the middle of the bed like a pale blue Halloween ghost. She stood as her small feet sunk into the mattress, her toes nimble enough to aid in balancing, and her mother was quietly out of sight. She stood there for she wasn't sure how long. Suddenly, the sheet lifted, way above her head like it was the sky again. As it did, Niya saw her mother cradling the corners, sending the sheet upwards to new heights, smiling at her. Niya laughed, she laughed a thunderous crackle and began to jump with her hands raised and body twisting in uncomfortable joy. She jumped and laughed, and soon, her mother laughed with her. Niya wasn't sure how the encounter ended, the last thing she remembered were her mother's eyes. The way they smiled and filled with joy and a temperament so soft she didn't seem like the same person to her daughter. She'd never seen them look like that, and couldn't remember a time they had since.

Niya rubbed her hand against the right wall, feeling up and down for the switch. She couldn't find it. The memory tingled then; it was on the other side. She recalled talking to her father about it, how it must have been an installation error to put the light switch next to the hinges of the door. She couldn't believe anyone would do something that inconvenient on purpose. Niya felt around the room, her hands tracing the outline of the darkness, and then touched and slowly pulled the door back. She felt around for the light, and in not much time, flipped the switch upwards.

Niya turned around, expecting the emptiness to act as a sort of relief to the clutter of the day, but was she wrong. The abundance of stuff in the room almost knocked her back. Piles of records and clothes covering every corner of the space. Had Niya ventured a little further into the room she would have certainly stubbed a toe or sent a long line of albums tumbling out of their scattered order. Niya examined the space, confused by the disarray, when she noticed the laundry basket, dirty-soled socks, and the half-empty cup of coffee on the nightstand. Niya inched towards the mug and knew that the guest room was no longer a barren space. She lifted the mug and smelt the still-potent coffee, mirroring the strength it always seemed to be when he'd drink it before bed. This was her father's room, and if Niya's recollection of the call she received was right, her mother found him dead in bed. So it wasn't only his new room, or the place of inside sky, not even the last place Niya remembered seeing her mother look happy. It was the room her father died in, and she knew, that was all it would ever be.

Part 2

Liddle Deaths

The slow-moving honey ran down the side of her mug and dragged towards the bottom like it was the last place it wanted to be. Its thick but thin drops decorated the cup with gold lines and dollops. Niya hadn't had a moment alone in the house since she arrived home for the funeral, until that morning. She touched her lips to the rim of the mug, only slightly, to blow wispy streams of steam out of her face. She looked out the window as she did.

The leaves weren't changing, yet Niya wished they had been. It would have made for a much more picturesque moment, maybe even an inspirational one. Her typical tea with honey, no lemon that day, gazing from the window of her childhood after her father's untimely death. It was exactly the sort of inspiration she needed to pick up a pen and write. She hadn't written anything since the eulogy. That, paired with her production input clause for the film, well, finding the time to compose an original idea just wasn't in the cards. She supposed that was why that moment in front of the window, blowing her too-hot tea, felt so special; she felt like a tiny piece of herself was escaping with the steam, her writerly self, needing to show itself to prove it was still there.

Niya's cell rang and was the perfect disruption to what felt like far too long of a five-minute moment of peace. She rarely had that luxury when visiting home, why should she now, even though her mother was still asleep. Niya lifted the phone and dreaded answering Colleen's call, but not as much as she dreaded seeing her mother after learning what she did the previous night. Not only were they sleeping in separate rooms, but Niya found out that her father died alone, and her mother, Anita, was planning on having her clean up the remnants. Niya swiped to green and accepted the call.

"Hey, Colleen," Niya spoke lowly. "What's up?"

"Hi, Niya. So sorry to bother you on a Sunday," Colleen sounded remorseful. "How'd it go yesterday?"

It had been all of one day since she received a call from her agent. Niya was genuinely surprised Colleen had paid her the courtesy of not calling on the day of the funeral. When Niya negotiated a producer title, she was unaware of the mounds of changes she'd ultimately agreed to sign off on. She had the ability to kill her darling, but the book to film process was beginning to feel like an over-zealous, horrendously bloody murder. The plot remained the same: two co-workers begin seeing each other before one begins to take off into professional stardom. Where it changed was in theme, Niya never considered her book a love story, it was one of hierarchy: workplace politics, race relations, pay inequity. Real things, not love. That's what Niya had convinced herself anyway. For the most part, that's how the book was seen by critics, an evaluation of ever unchanging professional bureaucracy. Whereas to most readers, it had become an in-depth, deeply involved story of unrequited love, according to numerous focus groups.

Niya was alright with it in the way a new kitten was okay with a bath. She knew it was going to be good in the long run, fat pockets never failed her, but the process was numbingly tedious. She found herself trying to hold on to pieces of dialogue, setting imagery, and other non-vital aspects that she knew the movie could go without. She hated having to agree to their removal though, having to swallow her now award-winning pride and admit that some things just didn't matter. There were a few days that Niya thought of backing out of the production gig, but Colleen convinced her that it'd be irresponsible as a creative, and just plain idiotic regarding those wide and fat pockets Niya talked about so much.

Recently, the film writers had been mulling over axing out a secondary character that Niya didn't find secondary: the protagonist's mother. She served as an outward consciousness for the protagonist, most of her revelatory monologues tumbling out while bearing all to her mother. They weren't sure she was necessary. Which Niya knew meant they weren't sure the monologues were necessary, and considering those were Niya's decidedly best pieces of dialogue and writing in the novel, she was having a hard time with accepting the red marker.

Niya began quietly fumbling around the kitchen in search of her car keys. "It was a funeral, Colleen. So it went about as shitty as it could've."

Colleen went silent. Niya knew the response wasn't called for, but she hated questions like that. She didn't buy the rejuvenating burial stories. Death was ugly and lonely, even when surrounded by hundreds of familiar strangers. Niya didn't think people should ask how putting a body in the dirt felt, she thought people should learn when to say nothing at all.

"Any news on the mom?" Niya asked, changing the topic.

"Yes, actually." Colleen seemed relieved. "They haven't set it in stone but seem to be pushing for her character to be replaced by the audience."

Niya squinted as she spotted her car keys in the distance, "So we're doing fourth wall breaking monologues now?"

Colleen exhaled, "It's not for certain."

"Well," Niya said as she put on her coat. "I'm just along for the ride, so if they feel it's for the best then they should go for it. I think it's a mistake though."

"I know you do."

"Her mother offered such textured and powerful matriarchy to that text," Niya shook her head. "Blows my mind. We can have an old and wise magical negro fixing white people problems, but not her own daughter's?"

Colleen became quiet again, so Niya said, "It's whatever, Colleen. Anything else?"

"Yeah," Colleen said with a slow-moving hum. "There's one more thing."

Colleen didn't say anything, so Niya probed. "What is it?"

Colleen hummed and hawed for another few seconds before she finally said, "They're thinking of changing the title."

A chill passed through Niya the way she imagined her father's spirit might. The producers had had their hands in everything, from pacing, character name changes, and apparent character eradication, but touching the title felt like a personal violation. The book was a best-seller and she'd been slapped with too many awards to keep track of. To change the name of a novel would mean to take away its identity, which was too ironic a concept considering it might have been the book's main theme. Niya stood still in the kitchen, car keys dangling from her fingertips and Colleen at her ear. She looked out the window again at the tree and wondered when something could be so changed, it was no longer itself. Niya wondered how much a thing could bend, how much it should have to, until it was no longer the thing it was supposed to be.

"No," Niya said, simply. "They can't change the title."

"It's not guaranteed," Colleen explained. "It was just a thought bouncing around the room. They thought shortening the syllabic count might be bene—"

"No," Niya said again. "There's only so far, Colleen."

Niya couldn't see her but knew she was nodding; it was all she could do.

"Anything else?"

Colleen replied, "Just don't forget about the virtual reading tonight. About a twenty-to-thirty minute read, then there will be a question and answer period. They're aiming for an hour."

"Got it."

"Do you know which chapter you're going to read yet?"

Niya lied, "Yup, I'm all set. I have a meeting to get to, Colleen. Talk later."

Niya hung up, and the lingering dread of combing the novel that night set on her shoulders like they were a perch, and the dread whistled a tune of inertia. She loved her novel, it was her pride and joy, everything Niya wanted her first hit to be, but the echoing nature of readings became prevalent nearly a month before. It was the repetition of the same sections and tongue twisting language being retold over and over, like that was the only thing she'd ever written. She remembered telling her dad about the way she'd been feeling. He was the only one she'd felt safe enough to talk to about it. She'd been doing readings and events for practically a year and knew she should still be on cloud nine. It was all such an honor, the dream of most authors, and there she was, tired of reading the same thing. Her father listened and grunted a few times, reassuring her that she was heard, and that she was understood. Niya wasn't sure which she appreciated more, because to be understood was a triumph within itself, but for her angst to be heard when all that she'd grown accustomed to people listening to was her writing, well, that was an achievement too. Nothing had seemed momentous about the things her father did though, not until now.

Niya left the house and got into her car. She selected the address that had already been input into her phone. It didn't feel like she had just been to the hospital a few days earlier, the whole sordid ordeal seemed like it was ages ago. She felt that was a common trope in the realm of grief. Like many of her day-to-day functions in mourning, her sense of time would just come to a halt. Actions and reactions would go unremembered, and it was normal to forget one's name for a second because the swelling memory of what was gone was just too consuming. Niya stepped on the gas.

The directions she followed triggered the recently formed memory of the first time she drove down this path. The bumpiness of side roads and bear right nudges pulled her back to when she had landed. Back to the town her father was no longer in. The place that all of a sudden felt even more distant than it once was. Fresh off the plane and her mother impatiently waiting, Niya gripped the wheel the way she did when she headed to the hospital not long before, steady and unsure.

This time, she didn't rush through the halls in confusion and mild alarm, she knew exactly where she was going. Niya had asked the medical examiner, Jerome Lacey, that they meet privately for the results a day or two after the funeral. She wasn't sure why she made it a secret, but a small drop of instinct worried that her mother wouldn't have been okay with what she was doing.

"The dead are dead," Niya pictured her mother saying. "Let them rest."

A piece of Niya could appreciate that, but another piece sought closure. When her mother blindly handed all the paperwork over to Niya after she had arrived at the hospital that first day, Niya swam through the forms. She recollected much of her father's information from memory rather than documentation, something she loathed doing. It was a prescription for stupid and unnecessary mistakes, but they were dropped on her lap, and the immediacy of the situation was unspoken but clear.

As she sorted through the confirmations of death, Niya saw it, tucked in near the back of the loosely-stacked pages and dog-eared forms, spousal signatures were required. She saw the autopsy consent confirmation. It was the neatest and shortest form of the bunch; it almost looked like a page of poetry; its use of white space immaculate. She touched the two empty check boxes on the form, the amalgamation of what life seemed to be at that moment: did we want to know what killed us, and did it really matter? Before clicking her pen and confirming what she was almost certain her mother wouldn't have, Niya thought of her lifeless father and shook her head. The image of him, so full of all life had to offer, succumbed to brittle bones and flesh. Niya had to know exactly what killed him. They figured as a result of his age and lifestyle, a stroke or heart attack was the culprit, but she needed to know. The decision shouldn't have had to have been a secret, but Niya knew her mother.

Niya approached Jerome's office door and saw that he was already seated. She glanced at him, intensely studying one of the dozens of looseleaf on his desk, his gaze fixed on the page the way hers would be when she wrote. He seemed too young to be bald, Niya thought, he couldn't have been much older than her. He wore it well though, a bronzed and buffed shaven head reflecting the awfully lit luminescence of hospital lights paired with his upright posture. Niya adjusted her twists and brought a few strands of hair forward before she caught herself in the motion.

Niya knocked on the door and quickly locked eyes with Jerome. A look of recognition washed over him which caught Niya off guard. Their initial meeting consisted of a few seconds as she popped her head into his office, similar to the way she was now, and to request the result meeting.

"Aniya," Jerome stood. "Good to see you again."

He gestured to the chair in front of his desk, and the two sat down, almost in unison. Niya gripped the base of her rental car keys and suddenly became nervous. Maybe her mother's imagined skepticism was well directed. What good would it do to know that he didn't suffer, if it meant you might find out that he did?

"How've you been?" Jerome asked, folding his hands together. He expressed concern in a way that she should have expected, but Niya wanted to roll her eyes the way she did with Colleen. She grimaced and took a mental note for an essay that she would write on the necessity of discovering what could be and should be said when greeting the mourning. *How've you been* just wasn't cutting it.

"I'm alright, thanks." Niya forced a smile. "So, what did you find?"

She was ready to get to it. Ripping off the band-aid as it went. Niya lost her aptitude for small talk about a year after merging into the professional world. The forced niceties and unnecessary catch-ups that never changed the cutthroat reality of the majority of work environments she'd encountered. What was the point? To make matters worse, she was Black and a woman in these spaces, so the eventuality of her being a per-ceived-confrontational-B was at hand. It didn't matter how she tried to problem solve or deescalate a situa-tion, the other aspects spoke too loudly, and she'd be perceived as the problem even if she wasn't. So, Niya had just stopped speaking unless she had to, and she found she preferred it.

Jerome grabbed the clipboard from the side of his desk and said, "Well, nothing unusual. He suffered a stroke, likely in his sleep, which I believe was noted?"

Niya nodded as Jerome continued, "Okay, it looks

like the primary cause was his hypertension brought on by the Liddle syndrome and there isn—"

"Little what?" Niya interrupted, sure she had heard incorrectly.

"Li*dd*le syndrome," Jerome slowed his enunciation down.

Niya searched her memory bank for the term. She searched the times she spoke with her father about medical history and doctors' appointments, but there was nothing. She would've remembered this; it epitomized the oxymoron far too well. Liddle sounded like little, and anything associated with a syndrome automatically felt momentous. It almost rang like a joke to Niya, Liddle syndrome, like a lesser form of someone experiencing a little death and the irreverence of what that meant to the institution of life. A small part of her wanted to chuckle, but a much bigger part sunk into itself. This was the second not-so-little thing Niya had discovered about her father over the course of two days after his death. She feared for whatever else might be looming in the memory of his recently-formed ghost.

"What is it? Something he had?" Niya asked, still processing.

Jerome tried to fight the slight frown Niya spotted twitching near his high cheekbone.

He replied, "Yes, I'm surprised he never mentioned it. It's a hereditary disease that causes severe hypertension from a fairly early age in anyone that's diagnosed. A lot of people don't find out until well into adulthood, but they were likely dealing with high blood pressure as early as their teens."

"I mean," Niya paused, still trying to wrap her head around things. "I knew he had high blood pressure, his doctor started him on meds for it some years back, but you're saying he's had this since childhood?"

Jerome nodded, "Did he go to the doctor often?"

Niya shook her head and whispered, "Rarely."

Jerome put the clipboard down and positioned himself away from the desk, leaning back into his chair as to signal Niya that the conversation was about to become much less formal.

Jerome asked, "Did your dad ever used to get dizzy spells? Was he tired often? Suffer from headaches?"

Niya didn't have to search hard for this remembrance, "No dizzy spells, but the others... I never thought much about it though. He worked long hours, of course he was tired. But the headaches, I never really thought twice about them."

Niya began a sort of reflection montage as Jerome went on about things she was no longer listening to. She thought about all of the times headaches or migraines would overcome her father. In the heat, after work, at dinner, before bed, while fishing, watching TV, listening to her read, while squabbling, at sporting events, when relatives visited, when relatives didn't visit, when he was awake, and Niya now wondered if he even had them while he slept.

"I can't believe I didn't notice." She stared blankly at Jerome, looking through him more than looking at him.

"Most people don't," he attempted to comfort her. "What matters is that he got on medication when he did."

"What if he had gotten on them before?" Niya asked. "If he had started on the medication earlier, could it have curved this?"

Jerome became uncomfortable, visibly and quickly. His jaw tensed and shoulders stiffened, Niya even swore she heard him grind his teeth.

He replied in a lower voice than he'd used before, "I can't say for sure, Aniya."

"But he was still a relatively young man, mid-six-ties. People live with high blood pressure way longer than that."

Jerome's discomfort was shifting to Niya. She crossed her ankles tightly and fidgeted in a manner only she could notice. The back of her knees suddenly became damp, and her anxiety focused on what would be the next thing to come from Jerome's mouth. He leaned forward again, meticulously intertwining his fingers the way he did before.

"This wasn't your fault," the words Jerome whispered sounded rehearsed and cliché. "You didn't know—you couldn't have known—"

Niya gripped her bag and stood in an unintentional fury, not knowing what else to do. She felt a sensation come over her, the same one that paralyzed her at the reception the day before. This time, she refused to stay frozen in place like some helpless thing sucking the pity from everyone in a mile radius.

"Thank you, Jerome," Niya said. "I have to get going."

"Aniya," Jerome stood as well, beating Niya's attempt at a hurried exit. "I get off early on Tuesday. We could talk more if you'd like."

Niya, already half-spun towards the door, glanced over her shoulder at Jerome, unsure if the invitation was out of pure concern, or something more. Niya looked down at her feet, her red sneakers popping in the white room in a way she hadn't noticed until then. Niya wondered if Jerome noticed her shoes. There was no right way to ask someone on a date, but this was definitely the wrong way. Or wrong time, as it were. So that couldn't be it, Niya assured herself.

He went on, "You might be up to talking a bit more then. How's three o'clock at the coffee shop right outside the hospital?"

A Tuesday, at three? He couldn't be. Niya didn't say anything. She looked up from her shoes and stared at Jerome.

"You don't have to answer," he quickly said. "But I'll be there at three if you're in the area."

Niya lifted the corner of her mouth and grinned softly as she headed out of the hospital, making a mental note of the location of the coffee shop and that he repeated he'd be there at three.

She arrived home shortly after, the conversation with Jerome the only thing on her mind. Her mother was up, messing with something on the stove. For a second, Niya thought she was making breakfast, but she was adjusting the knob, the one that was screwed on backwards, where low meant high, and high really meant low.

"Did you eat?" Niya asked, already knowing the answer. "It's been days, Mom. You have to eat something."

Anita ignored Niya's question and comment before she asked, "You get started on that room yet?"

"You mean last night?" Niya slumped down into the furthest chair from the stove. "When I was going up to bed?"

Her mother only looked at her before Niya continued, "No, Mom. I didn't clean out the room Dad died in on the day of his funeral."

Anita turned her focus back on the knob, "Well get to it now."

Niya watched her mother silently. She wondered if there was ever a time another person could make her feel the way her mother did. She imagined her father could have, had he been a cold-blooded raptor, but Niya could think of no one else. Her brooding began to swell and bubble up inside, forcing its way from her throat like lava out of a spigot.

"Are we going to talk about the fact that you and Dad were sleeping in separate bedrooms?" Niya shrugged. "Or no?"

Anita turned around and replied, "What's there to talk about? If you came home more than once every five years, you'd have known for a while."

"Five years?"

Anita rested her hips against the front of the stove while Niya sat up in her chair. The morning light was still potent and shone through the kitchen window, its whitish-yellow reflected off the cutlery, linoleum-painted floors, and stark white appliances. Both Anita and Niya lost sight of the other for a moment and only saw the light between themselves rather than the woman staring back across the kitchen.

"What happened?" Niya finally questioned.

Anita responded, "Nothing that hadn't been happening your whole life. Your daddy ain't here anymore, so you don't got to keep pretending like you didn't see that for yourself."

Anita turned around, giving Niya her back the way she often would and started fiddling with what Niya was sure was an unbroken knob. If Jacob was still around, that would have been one of his tension breaking moments. Some unnecessary anecdote or random work story to wash over the dry feeling in a room full of people. Now, empty was all the room knew how to be.

"I'll go get started on Dad's room," Niya said to Anita as she stood.

Anita didn't respond.

Niya climbed the stairs in apprehension of the room that was no longer spare, the smell of her father heavy and the feel of his possessions frightening. Walking back into that room would make it all real again. Niya found comfort in the distance between their home and the graveyard; it put more space between them. It was the least she could do—boxing up the remnants of a life shoved into a guest bedroom like it didn't belong in the home it swam through for a quarter century. She knew she had to organize his things before boxing and taking them anywhere, so as she inched towards the door, she made a conscious effort to breathe from her mouth while inside. If she couldn't smell the stale coffee or dried sweat stains from his shirts, he would still just be a memory, a distant body beneath soil. If she couldn't smell him, he wouldn't seem as real as she knew he no longer was.

Part 3

The Reading

Niya had looked at nothing other than the four walls of the guest room most of the day. Finally, being in her old room offered a much-needed sigh of relief. She and Anita hadn't spoken since morning, nothing but confirmation on the carpool for the next day, so Niya hadn't told her mother about the reading she was about to give. She watched the virtual count rise into the hundreds as Colleen texted her unnecessary notes of good luck. The routine had become second nature to Niya and luck was no longer required. She was introduced by the host and reached for the dog-eared page of her novel.

"Thank you all so much for joining us tonight," Niya smiled at all of the muted applause on her laptop and opened her book.

She was about to crack the spine, ready to recite one of her most read excerpts: an interaction between the protagonist and her love interest co-worker who run into each other after months of not speaking—clean writing, good metaphors, and a few laughs: Niya's recipe for reading comfort. Before she started, Niya stopped herself, recollecting on the happenings of the day—mostly, on her conversation with Colleen. Niya put her book down and minimized the view screen, quickly scanning her files for a piece that all of a sudden seemed like the one piece of writing Niya had that was worth reading.

Niya cleared her throat, "I had something selected, but it doesn't feel quite right tonight."

Niya was sure Colleen's panic attack had begun as she felt her phone vibrate repetitively on her knee, like tiny indecipherable knocks from that one overzealous neighbor, but Niya knew it would all work out, so she continued with her new plan anyway.

"The piece I'm going to read for you all tonight was actually on the cutting room floor during the editing process," Niya smiled as if on cue. "So, you're all getting a real exclusive tonight."

The intrigue of the virtual group heightened as Niya continued, "The section was a memory that Tulie shared with her mother about her grandmother. It's similar to some of the other moments she shares with her mother, but in this section, we explore her relationship with a character outside of the scope of the novel. My editor ended up pulling it because it felt unnecessary to the plot, but sometimes I think I should have fought harder for it. I mean, what's a plot without understanding the moments that make your protagonist who they are?"

Niya cleared her throat again, her cellphone no longer buzzing, and commenced:

Mebba told me once that in the South, Magnolia trees mean something different—to our people, anyway. Their stock and branches, thick and twisted between delicately soft blooms that almost make the trees seem beautiful. Almost. I visit her every summer, but this one has been quieter, more still. We still walk and talk like nothing is changed, but the house doesn't feel as comfortable under my toes. It often seems so alive, beating to invisible rhythms that polish the wood with the presence of too many guests and kind strangers that smile and tell me I look just like my grandmother.

"Grandmother?" she would shout whenever she'd hear the term. "Can a grandmother do this?"

And then she'd swing her hips something fierce to that same invisible beat that I knew she could hear too. She'd hitch up her skirt, well above her knees, and shake her derrière —a French-speaking man from another part of the world that came to visit Mebba told me that was a more elegant way of saying ass. I tend to agree with him now that I'm older, but back then, it was just another word I couldn't remember how to pronounce. Things don't seem as real when you can't pronounce them. She'd shake her derrière from side to side, lowering herself towards the ground as the guests of the house would chant and cheer and grind their own bodies the way Mebba would move hers. She'd stand slowly, her back inevitably knotted and tightened, but she'd never complain. Then if it was hot, which it almost always was, she'd wipe the sweat off her brow, as would all of the people I was yet to know. Their faces glistening, smiles and teeth shining with embers of brown skin, deep oak panels and floorboards flying around in a suffocating warmth that made me feel full instead of out of breath.

With her hand on her hip she'd say, "Ain't no grandmothers here." Then she'd laugh so unapologetically, the room would hum in a milky pleasure, and anyone there would be compelled to join in, not because they had to, but because something inside them told them it was okay to. My grandmother's name is actually

Melba, but when I was four and she, some half century older, decided she didn't want to be a grandma. So, she's a Mebba.

I've been here all of two weeks and not a single guest has stopped by to visit. I considered asking her about it, but I've come to know her as someone who does things in her own time, in her own way. So, we sit and talk and cook and listen to jazz, and I trust that this is exactly the way she wants things to be. That she wants some quiet and still.

"Tulie," she calls. She gave me the nickname as a baby, said that my face was shaped like a blossoming tulip and that I was the most spectacular bloomed bulb she'd ever seen take root.

"Let's go pick some apples," she says, pushing up from the sofa, her movement labored but fluid.

I'm inclined to go to her, to help her get on her feet, but I don't want her to start dancing, so I follow closely behind as she puts on her wide-brimmed hat and motions to the apple basket. I watch her fingers wobble as they unlatch the chain lock, the lines of her hands matching the peeling paint edges trying to hold on to the door frame. The back door is known to stick. Usually, she'll pry it open in a fury, like she has something to prove. She doesn't open it fast today though, she works through the knob, turning it in its entirety to a point where we hear something click. I didn't know that door clicked. She pulls it gently, and the door falls open in a way that looks like it's falling apart, like the pork from the night before fell off its bone, delicate and subtle. We walk together, and Mebba takes hold of my arm as we head down the dirt path towards the apple trees.

"It's mighty hot today," she says.

"No hotter than usual," I reply.

Our steps are in perfect unison; I have slowed down some and find myself grinning as we ease on down the road.

"It don't have to be hotter than usual for it to be hot, Tulie."

I nod and shrug, "I guess that's tru—"

Mebba stops walking, the abruptness pulls my arm back, impeding on the musical momentum.

"What's wrong?" I ask.

She doesn't answer. She is looking down, so my eyes follow her line of sight, and I know why she stopped. Not two feet in front of us is a copperhead. Its body coiled and neck upright like an image that came to life. We'd see snakes out here, footlessly running through the brush like excited children; it was perplexing. I knew snakes to be silent, stealthy, but behind Mebba's house they were free, and slithered like freedom meant something different there. Usually, when we'd run across a venomous one, Mebba would immediately pull out her axe and take it to the snake's head. The first time I saw her do it something heavy fell into my stomach. Seeing the snake's head off its body was only a part of it. I think it was seeing Mebba cock the axe over her head. The purposefulness of its descent, how unflinchingly she killed the copperhead. I'd seen her swat at flies and shoo spiders but never kill a thing like that.

When I asked her why she had to kill it, she said, "They'll get you if you don't get them."

I suppose that's the thing about killing. Everyone can have a reason.

Mebba doesn't have her axe now. My eyes lift off of the snake's dully burnt scales and back to Mebba. She isn't moving. She is just watching the snake. Her pupils are dilated, and her breath is soft. I glance down at her hand, and she is making a fist, a tight one where her axe should be. I look back at her eyes and think maybe she can't remember the last time she felt so vulnerable. I turn away from her and feel the heavy apple basket hanging from my grasp. I know if I hesitate, I'll miss. So, I take a quick step towards the copperhead, and as my foot lands above the small rolling pebbles, so does the basket, directly on top of the snake.

I look at Mebba again, and she still isn't moving. I rattle my arm and rub it against hers as if to wake from a dream.

"What do we do now?" I ask, inching into her line of sight.

She blinks twice and looks at me with surprise, like I haven't been standing with her the entire time.

Mebba tightens her arm around mine and continues walking.

"We'll get the axe later. Take care of that ole copper and get the basket back. Let's go get our apples."

"But." I frown a bit. "We don't have anything to carry them in."

Mebba looks up at me, and I remember when I used to look up at her. She opens her hands wide, stretching her slim fingers apart, and then she winks. Our teeth peek through as the laughter pours from us, and we keep walking towards the apple trees.

There aren't enough trees for this to be considered an apple orchard. When I think of those, there are long rivers of leaning trees lining paths down acres of unkempt grass. Here, Mebba has nine trees that she planted when she and my grandfather bought the property. When they moved here, Mebba found a piece of her soul in the land. Her land. Something no one in her or my grandfather's family had ever been able to say. So, she planted flowers and herbs and bushes and trees; she planted everything that could give what was hers, life. To breathe easy was what she called it, her love of gardening and nourishing the earth. She said it helped us all, to breathe easy. She planted a handful of apple tree seeds in a clearing behind the house, nine took. Even though there were so few, she still called it her orchard, and no one told her that it wasn't, because too much of the world already makes us feel small.

Mebba releases my arm and motions to the step ladder leaning under an especially crooked tree. I open it and climb a step. I know how to pick the apples she likes now. Extra firm and smooth to the touch. I wrap my fingers around some, squeeze them and trace my fingers around their skin. I do it by touch. I can tell by the grooves circling their sides if they've been battered or are still too young. When I feel them, I know, and I pull harder than I need to because I don't want to pull again. The snake has the basket, so I feel for five or six good ones.

She asks as I pass her the first apple, "You been having fun this summer, Tulie?"

"Always." I grin at her. "It's been quiet, though."

I roll my fingers against another apple, its skin is sharp, so I take it.

Mebba answers, "I know it has, but I thought it'd be nice to spend some time—just you and me."

She takes the second apple as I say, "Any particular reason?"

She pauses. I grab hold of a third apple and lower it to her, but she doesn't take the fruit. I look at her and see that she is looking right at me. She still hasn't responded. Her eyes are full and wet but not from tears, I don't think, but from something that makes her feel like the copperhead did. She's looking at me and holding her hand in a fist again. She wants her axe, but this time, only Mebba knows why.

"Mebba?" I lift the apple higher and watch her blink twice the way she did before.

"Sorry, baby." She takes it. "What did you say?"

I want to ask her what's going on, but I don't.

I repeat myself, "Is there any particular reason you wanted this summer to be just you and me?"

A wave of remembrance floods her face as she nods, and I feel for the fourth apple.

"Oh, no," she says. "I just thought it'd be nice. So much of my life has been a full house and parties and too many people. Sometimes I forget that just spending time with someone you love can be a party all on its own."

She sort of bobbles her head in a fun-loving way as she takes the fourth apple. Her pockets are becoming full.

"What do you mean, your life has been?" I ask. "Don't you mean is?"

She rolls her eyes as she points to an apple that I take as the fifth and says, "Has been, is, you know what I mean."

I step down, and she holds the fifth apple near her face.

Mebba says, "I thought you had to take bites out of life the way you would an apple. But I ain't got no teeth now, so I can't bite it the way I used to."

I chuckle as I put the step ladder back, and she says, "But baked apples taste sweet too, don't they, Tulie?"

I nod. "Even sweeter."

She smiles at me with her eyes, and I feel like I see her whole life in them. The wonder and joy and sadness and fear and music. I sometimes think that only older people can really smile that way, that in order to smile from your eyes you have to be able to smile from the soul. And that has to be a deep, deep, happiness, many years in the making. She touches my cheek and pats my face like I'm her little tulip again. She pats my face, and her eyes still smile, and I can't imagine a world without her.

"Let's keep walking," Mebba says as she walks past the trees and further away from the house.

I don't move, knowing the only thing further than the apples was not a good place.

"Do we have to?" I call out to her.

I know she can hear me, but she keeps walking. I close my eyes and let out the breath before looking back at the house. When I look back, Mebba has already turned the corner. I don't want to go, but I do anyway. I drag my feet and feel the blades of grass whip the tips of my shoes as I kick my foot out harder. I turn the corner and see Mebba approaching her orange lawn chair. She's moving quickly because by the time I get next to her, she is sitting comfortably in that uncomfortable chair right beneath the one tree she didn't plant on the property.

"I don't like it back here," I say.

"Neither do I," she replies.

I look at her as I lower myself to the ground. "So why do you insist on sitting back here, Mebba?"

I glance upward at the over-reaching branches of the Magnolia tree and shudder at how much they look like a hand, with the sky as a backdrop, inching downward to close in on us both. The flowers aren't in bloom anymore, and I like that whenever I come, they aren't. I don't want to know it as the almost beautiful thing I always heard about, but the haunting one that it still is.

Mebba looks out on the rest of her land where the corn used to be, and other things before it—tall, leaning, unwithered, and proud. It's flat now, but clean and bright and proud in another way.

"Because it reminds me of all the bad, Tulie," Mebba speaks in a low voice. "And that makes me appreciate the good even more."

She turns to face me. "When you've seen so much pain, you have to harvest the good things. Tend 'em, grow 'em, let yourself live in them, let them burst through and spoil you so good. But sometimes you have to know that the pain is still there, sit in its shade and let its cool breeze wash over you. Because when you ignore it, it doesn't mean it's not there. You got to learn to sit with it sometimes, let the shade make you stronger, then believe, even if you won't see it, that just like you can walk from under it, maybe y'all new babies won't have to feel it the same way. That maybe one day, all there will be, will be apple trees."

Mebba smiles, and I smile back. She continues, "I got something to tell you, Tulie."

"I know you do," I reply.

"My doctors say they found a bunch of polyps inside me," she whispers like it's a secret we're keeping from all the nobody around us. "They're small little flat bumps that can start growing inside you. They said I got a lot of them, probably had them for years. Don't know what it means yet though, could be nothing. Could be not nothing."

I listen and feel my heart begin to tap. It beats like it's running in place, trying to push forward but stuck in my limp body. I know this isn't bad news, but I also know it could be. My heart drops from my chest to my stomach, notching and contorting itself into a feeling I am trying to hide from Mebba. She is still talking, but I can't hear her.

Mebba takes hold of my hand and squeezes it with a strength I forgot she had. Mebba squeezes harder, and I squeeze back because I'm starting to under-stand. I sit and look out from under the shade of the Magnolia tree, feeling my hand in Mebba's. We sit like this for what I imagine are lifetimes, or just summers, and stare into the vastness of warmth around us. The tapping stops then, and my heart begins to feel as it should. Mebba seems to know and lets go.

"We should get back to the house soon," she says. "Do me a favor first, go get my axe from the house, and I'll meet you at the basket. Got to take care of that copperhead."

I nod and press my hand against the bark of the Magnolia tree and push myself to my feet. I don't move my hand though. I rub my palm and fingers up and down the body of the tree, feeling its dents and grooves embed themselves into the lines and spaces of me. I watch the color of my hand blend with the tree's and think of how we resemble, of all of the things we have in common. Then I take real notice of what I am feeling, the flat bumpy surface that occupies every part of what I am touching. I close my eyes and imagine I am touching Mebba, but on the inside.

"What if they weren't called Magnolia trees anymore?" I say as Mebba watches my hand. "Then maybe they wouldn't have to mean something different to us."

"Tulie, baby," Mebba says. "When Magnolias are in bloom, they're one of the most recognizable trees around. They can't be anything but Magnolia trees."

I spread my fingers against the bark one last time, my fingerprints carving in tiny pieces of me I didn't intend to leave behind.

"But if you look closely, when they're not in bloom," I whisper this time. "They look like they could be called Polyp trees, and that wouldn't always have to be bad, would it?"

Mebba nods as her eyes smile again, more fully than the time before. Her mouth smiles too, and all that beams from her in this moment make me feel like we are exactly where we need to be—my hand pressing against the past and its familiar ridges still fitting too well and Mebba's eyes cast in the shadow of the Polyp tree.

I start to walk back to the house and think of stopping to tell her that I love her. I glance over my shoulder, and she is looking out onto the field of nothing again, so I stay quiet and keep walking because I know she already knows, and right now, she needs to sit under her tree.

I am passing the basket and quicken my pace. Just knowing the copperhead is under there hurries me. I can see the house now, clear as day, but I stop. I stop and glance next to my feet. I'm parallel to the basket. It's so deceiving, sitting here in this unassuming way. It almost looks normal. Almost. It almost looks like it's just a basket. I step towards it and feel the tapping begin again, but these steps don't feel like the baby steps, they just feel like taps—deep and heavy ones that ricochet against my spine. I take notice of the rolling rocks again and feel unstable as I take my final step. I am above the basket. Looking down and picturing what's beneath looking up. I kneel and place my hands on each corner, gripping its rough wood and twine. I think of counting down from five because it feels like something I need to do, but things don't work that way. I consider counting down because I'm scared and think that'll make it easier, until I'm at one and realize that it won't. I feel the taps on my spine and exhale.

I crack the basket upwards on the side I cannot see. In not even a second, the copperhead slithers with the speed of something bigger, its body curving from side to side so quickly into the grass, it doesn't look like a snake anymore. It just looks gone. I pick up the basket and head back to Mebba, sure she'll be concerned I did what I did. But I already know what I'll tell her, and it'll be the truth, and I know she'll understand, because I do. I'm just not sure I'd like what the copperhead's death would mean, hidden amongst all of the, almost, beautiful trees.

Part 4

The Will

Wilbur Tessman's office was just as stuffy as Niya imagined it would be. She didn't frequent lawyers' offices, but had visited her fair share examining contracts, copyright agreements, and other new dustings that fluttered in with her recent literary success. There were always too many papers, files, or books stacked on their desks. It was as though they were obligated to clutter their workspace. Niya wondered if the cliché had manifested itself into an expectation. She had just gotten off the phone with Colleen, who was still praising what she called a *stellar and moving selection* from the night before. Colleen let her know she'd keep her posted throughout the day when Anita disgruntledly elbowed Niya in her ribs. Niya almost dropped her phone.

"What?" Niya snapped, Colleen still on the line.

Anita darted her eyes at Niya and asked, "Can this one thing not be about you? Just for today?"

Niya was taken aback; she hung up immediately and noticed the contempt in her mother's eyes.

"He's not even back in here yet, Mo—"

"Does that matter?" Anita interrupted. "We're reading your father's will. It don't matter if he's here yet or not, he's coming. Can't the rest of the world wait… for this?"

Niya wanted to shoot brimstone back at her mother. She wanted to pelt it at her along with her belief that the real reason Anita couldn't stand her success was because *she* made everything about herself. Whether it was the necessity of a new hat for church every month or her refusal to acknowledge her daughter's accomplishments, Anita always felt small when someone else felt big. So, to hear that from her shot Niya into a pessimism bordering on fatalism, and sitting there in Wilbur Tessman's office, surrounded by stacks of messily unfolded documents and never cracked books put Niya even more on edge.

"Sorry about that." Wilbur hurried back into the office as off-balance as when he left. "Let's get started."

Wilbur sat down, and Niya finally tore her eyes off of Anita as he said, "Well this is definitely an intimate group. You'd be surprised at how many people I've had to squish in this office. Sometimes I feel like I barely fit, even without eleven clients."

Niya could see that Wilbur was waiting for someone to laugh, his forced and awkward smile, the hesitation in continuing his thought. Normally, when Niya was with her mother, she'd succumb to the social niceties she detested, but not that day. There was still too much smoke building in her, she worried the smile might set it loose. Anita didn't flinch. They watched Wilbur's attempt at lightening the mood fly by as his smile melted.

"Alright," he said. "Let's get to it."

He began with the mundane—the brass tacks of his duties and other essential portions of the process Jacob had gone through. Wilbur informed Niya and Anita that when his will was signed, Jacob was of sound mind and body. Niya held a poke of laughter back amidst the smoke still inside her. She and her father would laugh at terms such as 'sound mind' in a culture like theirs, one where the concept of sanity was subjective and influenced by class, race, socio-economic standings, and too many other undiscussed factors. Jacob said to Niya once, *if we can accept that we live in a world where gods exist and equality doesn't, then we all must be a bit batshit*. Niya couldn't help but smile when he swore around her; it made him seem more tangible, less like a father and more like a person. Niya glanced at her mother sitting next to her in the office, her strong jawline and smoothly rounded nose and wondered what tangible thing there was between them. If they'd ever be more than mother and daughter, if they ever had been.

"Everything is pretty straightforward," Wilbur stated while examining the paperwork. "Jacob didn't have many assets to divvy up between the two of you. He had an insurance policy that he started paying into some years ago in the amount of twenty-five thousand dollars. This has been willed to his wife, Anita Lewis."

Niya saw her mother nod and let out a small grin from the corner of her eye before Wilbur continued, "Then there's the matter of his 401k, in which you were both his beneficiaries."

Wilbur began rifling through a file before pulling out a yellow form or receipt.

"The confirmed statement I had sent over is for two hundred and two thousand seven hundred and thirty-six dollars, which will be split evenly between the two of you."

Niya took a mental note of the hundred thousand and began brainstorming the possibilities surrounding her father. She thought about establishing a fund or scholarship in his honor, but she knew the thing that would tickle his fancy would be having his name smack dab in the middle of some monstrosity. She thought of the community center he'd given so much of his time to the past few years, pulled out her phone, and made a note to look into naming rights. She didn't see the appeal in that sort of commemoration, but even though he would have never admitted it, her father was a glamorous man. Both of her parents were. Anita wore it in her style, accessories, and not-so-clear-cut vanity; Jacob revealed it in his need to be adorned. His longing to be idolized, not by the masses, but by the few people in his life that he thought mattered. Niya second guessed herself then. Maybe he wasn't so glamorous, maybe he just wanted to be seen. Or to sparkle, just a bit. He'd soaked up all of her success and radiated with a type of pride Niya didn't really think twice about. It's how a parent should feel, she thought. Her success was his success, her achievements were his achievements. Niya started to realize that Jacob might have adopted that attitude out of a need for fulfillment, not parental pride, because what was a life without success? What would life be to someone that desperately sought to be seen, if he thought there was nothing special to look at?

"And finally," Wilbur cleared his throat and paused. "The deed to the house."

Wilbur hesitated. His silence flagged Niya, and though she didn't know what exactly, she knew they were suddenly on course for something stirring.

"Unlike the monetary assets," Wilbur went on. "The deed has been allotted to just one of you: Aniya Lewis."

An actual chill swept through the room and numbed Niya. She wanted to look at her mother but was sure it wouldn't result in anything but a speedier descent into the hell she knew was coming.

"Come again?" Anita asked.

Wilbur noticeably gulped.

"The deed was put in Aniya's name as of," he paused, squinting down at the paper, "three years ago. It was the last change he made regarding his wil—"

Anita interrupted, "That son of a bi—"

"Mom," Niya quickly cut her off.

She had never heard her mother use the term. Niya almost felt like Anita had slipped on it, been taken so off-guard she didn't even see it coming. She'd spent so many years of her life condemning profanity, Niya had forgotten that oftentimes with her mother, what happened outside of the church stayed outside of the church. It was a built-in hypocrisy she had learned from her mother and many, but not all, others when it came to religious ethics: you didn't have to practice what you preached, not when it didn't suit you. It was a lesson that began small, and as the scope of Niya's life grew, so did her understanding of that fact. Everyone's a saint until they ain't.

"There has to be something we can do about this," Anita said sternly. "That's my house. The home I've taken care of for almost thirty years. Do you know how much I've put into that house? He can't just give it away."

"Well, Mrs. Lewis," Wilbur replied, and Niya recognized the sudden formality. "The deed was passed down to Mr. Lewis by his parents after their passing, and in a note I made per our last conversation about the change, he said, 'I want to be able to leave something for my daughter the way my parents were able to leave something for me. I don't have much, so it'll have to be this.'"

Niya felt the tears well up, but she held them in so surely, they started to burn. It sounded just like him, through and through. Wilbur glanced at Niya, nearly as touched by the sentiment as she was, and quickly revealed a small smile in the memory of his client. For the first time since Jacob passed, Niya didn't feel so alone in a room with her mother.

"Bullwash," Anita cut through the sentiment like a blade. "He changed that when things got worse. None of that is true. That's my house."

Niya listened to her mother's tirade progress as her anger bubbled out into the already warm and stuffy office. Niya didn't look at Wilbur—she couldn't—she was embarrassed. She knew she shouldn't be; if Anita's actions had ever showcased anything, it was that she made her own choices. This blow-up was no different. It didn't matter that Wilbur was just the messenger of a dead man or that that dead man happened to be her husband and these his final wishes or that their daughter was sitting not even two feet away, still mourning, gripping the arms of her chair because it was all she could do to hold herself up. None of that mattered; nothing else ever mattered.

Anita eventually stopped to catch her breath, and Wilbur took the pause to jump in, "Mrs. Lewis, there really isn't much I can do for you now. You can seek legal support and contest the will if you so choose, bu—"

Anita clutched her bag and stood up, still and tense.

Anita snapped, "I will."

"That may be difficult," Wilbur attempted to explain. "You can take action, of course, but contesting it will be a drawn-out process, especially considering the length of time the changes were made before his death. That and other debatables."

"Like?" Anita asked.

Wilbur shrugged. "Various things that would make for an unobstructed case. Proof of financial contributions you made towards the home, an autopsy report confirming death of natural causes—"

"Liddle syndrome," Niya felt the words tumble out of her mouth. "He had Liddle syndrome."

Niya saw Anita's eyes narrow as Wilbur spoke, "I don't think I've heard of it."

Niya avoided her mother's gaze and replied, "It's a type of early-onset hypertension. He'd likely had it since his teens. The cause was natural."

"Oh," Wilbur said. "So, you had an autopsy done?"

"Of course she did," Anita whispered loud enough for both to hear, and before Niya could answer, she turned to face Wilbur. "I'll be in touch."

Anita walked out of the room with purpose. Niya heard her footsteps clearly and loudly as she headed down the hall. Niya pushed off the arms of the chair and let out a quiet sigh as she stood. She looked at Wilbur and nodded before averting her eyes from his. They were so full of pity, for her, her mother, and her father. Niya hated pity even more than she hated embarrassment, so she left almost as hurriedly as her mother did.

Anita was by the car when Niya exited the building, her arms crossed and her temperament unknown. Niya unlocked the door from a distance and approached the car after Anita was inside. She held her hand to the handle for too many seconds to count. Her instinct was flaring, fight or flight, but Niya was tired of fighting. She wanted to flee, to let go and just run in the opposite direction. She wanted to do anything but get in that car, but she had nowhere to run. The world was at her back, and Niya knew that the only place she could go was ahead of her, so she couldn't do that either. She stood frozen at the door for as long as she could.

Niya pulled the handle and flopped down into her seat in a surprisingly heavy way. The rental car bounced beneath them and slowly settled. Niya apprehensively awaited her mother's spiral to begin its descent again. Niya pulled out of the parking lot, driving more tentatively than when she was first learning. Her turns crept with an eerie howl, punctuating the tension. It all felt so silly, driving the way she was in her attempt to not disrupt what she believed was brewing, but she didn't stop. Niya drove as if there was a fragile thing being carried in that car, too much speed, noise, or sudden movement would be disastrous amidst its already undesirable state. Niya felt the gritty bumps on the tattered road and slowed down even more, gripping the wheel like it made a difference. She drove all the way home like that. Niya wondered if Anita feared for the fragile thing as well, if she sensed its presence the way her daughter did, as she too, hadn't uttered a sound.

Part 5

Keys

Anita disappeared into her bedroom as soon as the two returned home, and Niya slumped down on the plastic-wrapped sofa in the good room. She knew if Anita was around, she wouldn't dare drape herself over the furniture that way, but the plastic made it almost impossible not to. Niya would slide around on the Pepto Bismol-colored sofa, even as a kid, while attempting to find a position that wouldn't sink her towards the edge of the cushions. The furniture plastic acted as a natural lubricant against whatever clothes she was wearing as though the sofa refused to let anyone be comfortable. Even as guests poured in to mourn her father, Niya would watch them struggle and shuffle backward as the chair's gravity insisted on them being near to the ground. Anita would see it too, Niya knew, but the discomfort the chair caused everyone was no match for her mother's need to preserve a thirty-year-old paisley-patterned couch she was gifted by her own mother.

Niya didn't remember the story very well, but she knew the couch was given to her parents shortly after their marriage. Anita would go on about her mother's generosity, about how much it meant for her mother to give such an extravagant gift when she had so little. Anita had a wonderful relationship with her mother before she passed; the two were virtually best friends. They'd talk almost every day and visit whenever possible. The two had become even closer after Anita's sister died, the loss solidifying the bond between the two remaining members of their already small unit. The pink couch embodied all of that love bundled tight between the plastic wrap. Anita would go on about how long her mother must have saved up to buy it for them, how no one had ever given her something that meant so much. Anita had learned a little more about the story sometime later, about her mother trading in some old watch of her father's to get enough for the couch, but Niya was stuck on the details. She reclined and tried to recollect the story instead of worrying about the news Wilbur broke to them that morning.

She also thought of Anita's mother. Niya had a good relationship with her grandmother. She often wondered why the bond seemed to skip a generation. Niya would follow her through the brush and help with odds and ends around the house, but it was the stories that stood out to Niya. Her grandmother would tell her real stories Niya always figured were made up and made up stories that usually rang with more truth than she'd let on. She would become immersed in her grandmother's inflection and attention to detail. The turns of phrase and control of tension and pacing that gripped the listener all the way through the narrative. Her grandmother used tactics that Niya later studied during her MFA years, and she wondered how she was able to become so proficient at something that writers struggled to perfect. It seemed constant as Niya progressed in her career, the reminders of the ease some had in doing things that others strived to do. Niya wished her grandmother had been able to read her book, that she could have gone into a bookstore and seen her granddaughter's name donning one of the many texts that decorated the shelves. She knew it would have meant something to her, like it meant to her father, like she wondered, if it ever meant to Anita.

As Niya shifted around in her seat, she was caught off guard by a knock at the door. It was still fairly early in the day, and with the funeral service passed, Niya thought most of the stray visitors had ceased with their check-ins and stop-bys. Niya twisted herself out of the plastic divot she had formed in the sofa and found her footing before hurrying to the door. Her parents didn't have a peephole, which constantly unnerved Niya, so she slightly cracked the door and poked her head just outside instead.

"Hi," the kid standing there sort of shouted. "I'm De'Quan. My grandpa and Mr. Jacob used to work together, and he was fixing up an old Honda Prelude for me."

Niya opened the door the rest of way. "My father passed away recently, so I don't thin—"

"Oh, I know," De'Quan interrupted. "We were at the funeral; I'm sorry for your loss."

Niya nodded. "Thanks. But I don't know anything about a car."

"He had it ready months ago," De'Quan explained. "He was just holding it for me so I could save up the rest of the money. He already signed the title over to me and everything."

De'Quan pulled an envelope from his back pocket

that was overflowing with cash. Niya watched as the kid struggled to stuff a few of the pieces pushing out from the corners back inside.

"We agreed on five thousand," he said while handing the envelope to Niya. "It's all here, you can count it."

Niya lifted her hand and gently pushed the money back towards him. "Come in and give me a minute."

Niya showed De'Quan to the infamous pink sofa and watched him carefully lower himself onto it; he'd clearly sat on a plastic-covered chair before. His balance was pristine as he sat, back straight against the too-upright sofa and tightly tucked his knees inward. His cherry red high tops popped the same way Anita's lipstick would with their house as the backdrop. Niya darted upstairs and knocked on Anita's door. Had it been her father in the room she would have knocked and slowly cracked the door like she would at the front, but she dared not do that if her mother was on the other side.

"Mom," she said. "Do you know something about a Honda Prelude Dad was working on?"

Anita spoke through the door, "Out back."

There was no follow up or further explanation. Anita went silent, and Niya stood outside her door wondering if she was going to get anything else out of her mother.

When she realized she wasn't, Niya headed downstairs and asked De'Quan to follow her out back. She hadn't made her way to the back since she got there; she rarely did. There wasn't much of a yard, only enough space for a few trees and shrubs, because most of the space was taken up by the oversized shed her father had outfitted as his workspace-slash-garage. The shed was off to the right of the house, not obstructing any views or even visible through the back-facing windows. It used to be white but resembled a grayish-brown now. Niya had helped her father paint the shed over twenty years ago, and it hadn't seen a touch-up since.

Niya grabbed the keys from behind the old shovels Jacob kept against the side of the shed. She went for them without even thinking about it and knew that was the way her father would grab them. She thought of the hundreds of times he'd held those keys without even giving a second thought to how easy it'd be for someone to find them. Niya rubbed her finger over the key's rough pattern and felt she was likely rubbing some remnants of her father's skin cells into her own. She fiddled with the old lock and removed the chain before pulling the doors open.

Niya's hand hovered above her for a moment then brushed the hanging string she always struggled to locate. She pulled, and the light barely lit the dusky shed but shone bright enough for Niya and De'Quan to see the old Honda. It was the '99 model, and her father had painted the car matte black. The rims were a dull chrome, and the windows looked recently waxed. A bit of dust had settled over it, but the car was beautiful, as they all were when Jacob finished with them.

"Damn," Niya heard De'Quan whisper as he touched the taillight. "I wish I could have thanked your dad for this."

She grinned. "Let me grab you the keys."

Niya made her way to the driver's side door and pulled the handle with no luck. It was locked. She tried the passenger side, but it was locked too. Jacob usually kept the keys of the cars he was working on inside the vehicles—the glove compartment or dashboard, but they'd clearly been stored somewhere else this time. Niya looked around the shed at the abundance of make-shift shelves, containers, and half-stored boxes before deciding to send De'Quan home. She told him to come back in a few hours so she could look for the key and wipe the car down for him. Niya examined the space, attempting to order her search based on her father's logic. She found her way to his worktable and began searching through the small drawers loaded up with cloths, polish, and too many loose car parts for her to count.

Niya was seven the first time her father brought her into the shed to work on a car with him. Anita wasn't fond of the idea, believing Niya should be focused on something a bit more appropriate for a second grader, but Jacob said it was practical.

"These are life skills," he told her. "Ones that go far beyond a classroom."

Niya would sit cross-legged and watch him pull and prod at different things under and inside the cars he worked on. He'd get her to look at the car with him and pass him tools from time to time, but save the standard wrench, hammer, and pliers, Jacob didn't know the names of much of what he worked with.

"Pass that thing there," he'd gesture. "Give me that one with the round top."

Niya's observational skills began centering in that space she shared with her father, because none of the communication was verbal after a while. He'd nod in a general direction or vaguely motion to a pile of bolts he hadn't yet organized. It became Niya's job to decipher the gesture and find what he needed, and she got good at it. They'd work in tandem as he'd reach for some tool, and she'd already have it waiting for him. They were a team, and it was Niya's first experience being a part of one she thrived in. She didn't excel at sports or group projects at school, she mostly preferred working on her own and not having to depend on anyone to get where she was going—a trait she believed fed most of her writerly longings. Niya felt at a young age that depending on someone else meant to slow down in approaching the win. She thrived on her accomplishments, even as a kid, as did her father. Anita wasn't so impressed by awards and accolades—she told Niya she was more fond of good character. So, Niya continued to produce what she could control, what she could accomplish for a parent that was fond of work ethic and acknowledgement. She worked at being a winner, so her father could be one too. But it was also with her dad, working on remodeling cars, that she learned that being a part of a team was simply an extension of the qualities she already had. Whether it be her attention to detail or intuitive nature, Niya understood that by offering a small piece of herself she could be a part of something bigger. Something about that filled Niya with a hope she didn't know she needed, a hope she and Jacob had shared. She closed the drawers she'd sifted through and moved on to the boxes near the car.

The boxes were mostly filled with car parts, some still packaged and others half-open. Niya dug through the boxes in hopes that he'd dropped the key into one by accident like he'd done so many times before. She looked under and around the parts he'd collected that were likely pieces he had tried to fit to the Honda while working on it. Before she left for college, Niya had her own up close and personal experience with car part haggling when she went looking for a genuine Mercedes-Benz emblem. Jacob had been working on the '92 Mercedes for a few months and was approaching the finish line. His overhead was shot on the project when he realized he'd forgotten to buy a new emblem for the hood of the car. The value would go up if the car was fully restored, but he'd painted himself into a corner with the expensive project.

Jacob's birthday was approaching, and Niya hated shopping for her father as he never wanted or needed anything. That year, she knew there was something her father didn't have that she'd be able to procure. Niya saved up a hundred dollars and asked Anita to take her to one of the shops her father frequented, knowing they usually carried an array of emblems in a glass cabinet behind the counter. Niya asked the shop owner about the Benz emblem and to her surprise, was quoted nearly double the cost she'd known her father to get for similar items. The shop owner went on about the market, supply and demand, and how sought-after Benz emblems were. By the time they were done, Niya had managed to talk him down to a hundred and fifty dollars. She told the shop owner she'd be back, but when she returned to the car without the item, Anita chimed in.

"What do you mean he charged you more than the goin' rate?" she asked.

Niya replied, "He said he couldn't let it go for any-thing less."

Anita eyed the shop from the car window. "Give me your money."

"Mom, it's oka—"

"Give it!" Anita insisted.

Niya handed her the hundred dollars and watched her strut into the shop. Niya waited and knew that the deal she'd made was about to be obsolete. Anita had a way of pushing herself onto and into situa-tions she knew nothing about, and Niya was sure her attempt to bully the shop owner would equate in no more than a missed opportunity. Anita came out a few minutes later and fished a bag out of her purse after she sat in the car. She tossed it on Niya's lap and immediately revved up the engine. Niya knew it was the Benz emblem without having to look in the bag.

"How'd you talk him down?" Niya asked.

Anita didn't respond as she backed out of the parking spot.

"Mom," Niya said. "How'd you do it? That guy wouldn't budge."

"You ever heard the story of the rock and the wall?" Anita asked her.

"No."

"That's 'cus it ain't finished yet. They're both still there," Anita replied. "Don't ever accept what you know ain't fair, not if you can help it."

Niya gripped the emblem through the bag and the two drove home in silence. Later that week, she gave her father the piece of the Benz that would get him at least a few hundred more dollars.

He smiled and hugged her as he laughed out loud. "This is my kind of gift!"

Niya glanced at Anita on the other side of the room as she watched the two of them spin around on the carpet.

Niya had emptied all of the boxes near the car and still hadn't found the keys, so she meandered to the last place she figured they might be. In the corner of the shed, Jacob kept his battery-powered record player covered with a filthy cloth he used to protect it from the dirt and grime the shed produced. There was always a record inside. He would play it on repeat as he worked on a car, flipping it when he sat for one of the few breaks he took. Niya reveled in the Motown classics he would play. He'd sway from side to side as he worked, and the beat filled him. If cars were her father's first love, she knew music was a close second. He always talked about feeling the most like himself when he was working on a car, but Niya felt he acted most like himself while listening to music, poised and sure and funny and a bit goofy. She realized as she pulled the cloth off of the record player that she'd never danced with her father, and now she never would.

She lowered her head and let out a short breath when she saw them right next to the record player: the keys. Niya picked them up, but before going to the car, she noticed something leaning against the folding chair her father usually sat in. It was wedged between the seat and back, its white hue glowing in the dark corner. Niya pulled a book out from her father's favorite chair and almost lost her footing. Her knees locked as she looked at the stained cover of her own manuscript. Niya flipped through the pages and noted all the grease prints and dogeared sections Jacob had told her were his favorites. The book was so worn. Niya closed it and pressed the book into her stomach, its edges sharp enough to make her feel something other than grief. She put it down before dusting off the car and starting it up. The engine purred softly, the way her father had told her it was supposed to, and she sat in the front seat as proud of his achievement as she knew he did in that very shed for her.

De'Quan returned a little while later, and Niya handed him the keys.

"Thank you." he smiled while taking the keys and handing her the money.

Niya shook her head and said, "Keep it. I think he'd want you to have it."

De'Quan looked stunned, "I can't."

"You can," Niya said. "Just do me a favor...if you name it, call it Jacob."

De'Quan's eyes filled with more emotion than Niya had seen in a long time, which said something considering she'd just attended a funeral.

"Okay," he whispered. "I will. Thank you."

He got into the car and backed out slower than he needed to. He waved and honked at Niya as he drove off the way Jacob used to, sparkling and elated. Niya grabbed her father's copy of her book and closed the shed doors. She thought about leaving it unlocked, knowing there was nothing else of value in there for someone to take, but she chained it up anyway. Niya locked the shed and hid the keys deep under the shovels, almost as if she'd forgotten that he wouldn't be back to use them anymore.

Part 6

Hurt People

Niya spent most of the afternoon and night boxing her father's belongings in the guest room. She finished around two in the morning. She picked up a few mementos to take with her, her favorite being his stained coffee mug. Niya didn't drink coffee, she never got accustomed to the bitterness, but the smell was a sense memory of the morning chats she used to have with Jacob. Sitting over his blue mountain or ground mushroom blend, the smell of his coffee and her herbal tea would commingle and twist together through the kitchen. Sprinkles of soft greenery and harsh earthy aromas would dance around them, their laughter and intrigue. When Niya began packing up his room, she poured the remnants of what coffee

87

was left in the mug, but she didn't wash it. She stuck her nose deep down inside and filled herself with the scent of him, the scent of the memory, and it worked. When the odor penetrated her nose, she was sure, just for a second, that she heard his voice. His laugh. The sound filled her almost as drastically as the smell did, ground coffee aroma clinging to her nostrils for dear life. Every time she smelt it, her shoulders would ease and her back would open up; it occurred to her that she was just able to breathe again, truly and fully. Within his mug and the smell of too many conversations to count, Niya remembered how to breathe. More so, she remembered that she had to.

Niya and Anita hadn't spoken the entire previous day, but as Niya feared, the time of avoidance was drawing to a close. Niya heard her mother rustling around in her bedroom and figured it was as good a time as any; she needed to know what to do with the boxes. Niya's genuine concern over her mother telling her to throw his stuff away had been at the forefront of her mind since taping the last box shut. It stunned her, being able to so neatly pack up sixty years of life into a single space. A few of his trinkets were spread around the house, but it was mostly all there. Having everything he owned, save the house, equate to the contents of a single room pulled on something in Niya, scared her if she was being honest with herself. She knew that life was about the way someone lived it, and he lived even though there were times he didn't think he did enough, but he lived. In compassion and stories and laughter and love and fear and resilience and in cars and coffee and his daughter; and his daughter. Niya wished she had thought all of that through before he was gone, that she had told him just once that he lived beautifully, and how much it meant to her to have experienced parts of it with him. He'd always tell her how lucky he was to have her for a daughter. Niya wished that she had said it back, just once.

She was a few steps away from her mother's door when her cell buzzed. It was Colleen with another update.

Meeting scheduled early tomorrow morning for final decisions on 4th wall and title. Be in touch.

-C.

Niya hadn't thought about the film all morning. It might have been the longest time in the past six months she'd gone without it creeping back into her thoughts, plaguing her free time and peace of mind. Perspective seemed to shake that loose, and while she hated that it took a funeral to do it, Niya was relieved that she could step away again, even if it was just for a few days.

Niya tapped on Anita's door and called out, "Mom, do you have a minute?"

"Yeah," Anita replied, her voice hollowed by the door.

Niya stepped into the room and didn't recognize it. Everything was different. The bed, armoire, dressers, and vanity were all a richly dusted oak color. The shag rug was red and posh, as was the duvet paired with gold laced pillows. The room was stunning; the room was Anita.

"Wow," Niya finally expressed.

"You like?" Anita asked, folding a pair of corduroys. "I've been getting it piece by piece, staking out the Goodwill and some thrift stores out of town. Got the bed and dressers at a church auction. I'm almost done now. Just got to get a chest for my valuables and maybe some curtains."

Niya sat in the elegantly curved chair in front of the vanity. "It's really pretty, doesn't even look like the same room."

Anita nodded slightly. "I always wanted a room like this, but your daddy thought it was a waste of money. Nice things don't got to be a waste if they make you feel good. He neva' understood tha—"

"Can we not, Mom."

Anita stopped folding. "Not what?"

"Bash Dad." Niya crossed her arms. "Not today, at least."

"Bash him?" Anita threw the pants on top of the basket. "How is it bashing someone if it's the truth?"

Niya exhaled and closed her eyes; Anita went on before Niya was able to begin, "You see, that's the problem with you. The both of you. You never wanted to hear anything except what you wanted to hear about the other, like y'all thought each other was perfect or something. Well, you're not, and neither was he."

"Okay," Niya stood up. "I don't want to do this today. Can you just tell me what you want me to do with Dad's stuff?"

"Not today," Anita walked around to the front side of the bed. "Have you ever wanted to? When would it be better for you?"

"I don't know!" Niya raised her voice and threw up her hands. "Not three days after burying him."

Anita looked at her daughter, the same way she looked at her in the kitchen after the funeral. The same way she often did. She looked at Niya and sat down on the edge of the bed and continued folding clothes. Niya looked around in search of a set of eyes to meet to express her frustration, but the only other pair had begun focusing on laundry.

"Mom?" Niya wavered. "What do you want me to do with his stuff?"

Anita's face softened, and she cleared her throat slightly before beginning, "You know, I was planning to go to college before I had you."

"What?"

"College," Anita repeated. "I got accepted into two schools and was gonna go. I didn't know what I was going to study, but I was going. I would've been the first one to graduate."

"What are you talking about?" Niya asked, confused.

"You always go on about that," Anita said. "In all those interviews and shows, you always bring it up. That you were the first. Well, I could've been. But I had you."

"So, you're blaming me?"

"Did I say that?" Anita snapped. "I'm just telling you. We were a year out of school, your daddy and me, when we found out I was pregnant. I'd been working at the mill with your grandma, saving up to start classes that fall. And when I told your daddy, the first thing he said was we had to get married."

Niya raised her eyebrow. "Isn't that a good thing?"

"You tell me," Anita said. "You tell someone you're pregnant, and the first thing they do is tell you what you're going to do... That sound good to you?"

Anita paused and offered Niya a chance to respond, but she didn't, so Anita went on, "I told him that I had spoken to my sister. She was willing to help us. After I gave birth, she'd take care of you while I was in school and your daddy worked. But he didn't want to hear it. He asked me what that would look like, my sister, God rest her soul, taking care of our baby."

Anita emptied the rest of the basket onto the bed and kept folding as she continued, "He said he'd have no part in it. That we had a responsibility, so school was out of the question. I asked him what he meant when he said he'd have no part in it, and he looked at me and said, we either get married and raise that baby right, or we won't be together at all."

Niya's heart dropped. "He was just upset, Mo—"

"Too upset to take it back in a week?" Anita said. "Or a month? Or three months? Or for the rest of my pregnancy, for that matter?"

Niya sat back down as Anita said with a soft smirk, "Ah, he didn't tell you this story, did he? You ever wonder why he didn't have one of his great stories to tell you about the day you were born?"

Niya shook her head. "I don't want to do this, Mom."

"Because he wasn't there," Anita replied. "He never came; not even after I took you home. When you was about a month old, your aunt got sick again. The lupus was back again, and it was worse than it ever had been, she wasn't in no state to take care of a baby. So, one day when I was out, she called Jacob and told him she had something to talk to him about, and to come over and meet his daughter. When I got back, there he was, proud and stubborn as the day I met him. You know, he didn't even want to hold you?"

Niya's eyes began to well up again, but this time she didn't have the power to hold the tears in. Quiet streams fell so fast she didn't even realize she was crying. Anita watched her daughter's face flood before she picked up a pair of socks and kept going.

"My sister told him that she wasn't going to be able to help me the way she wanted to," Anita rolled the socks together. "So, he was going to have to come on back, do his job as a father. Jacob looked at me and asked, what'll it be? I stormed off into the kitchen and my sister followed me, she told me I didn't have a choice anymore. That she didn't want me to be like all of these other women out here struggling on their own. Jacob had a job, and a house, and could give us a life. She told me I didn't have any other choice. She said it over and over again. So eventually, I married him. Moved into this house. Forgot about school and kept working at the mill. My sister died a few years later, Jacob told me it was a good thing I made the choice I did, because if I didn't have him, I wouldn't have had anybody, anymore."

"What is this?" Niya wiped her face and chuckled. "An explanation? Your reason for treating me like this?" She stood up again, a similar bubbling sensation rising in her chest. "What do I know? Maybe he didn't want me in the beginning, but you didn't want me in the end."

"How dare you say that?"

"What?" Niya stepped closer to her mother. "The truth. I mean, it makes sense now. The reason you've always been so damn frigid, why you don't seem to give a crap about any of my accomplishments, school, jobs, books, nothing. You were jealous; you're still jealous. And now, you're even more bitter than you have been, so you're saying all of this shit to hurt me because he left me the house, not you."

"I gave up everything for you," Anita said. "Everything! Your father knew that, and the only reason he treated you like his little angel was because he knew what he had done. What he was prepared to do. A guilty conscience can last a lifetime. I told him that too, years ago, right before he moved into the guest room. Right before he changed that will. I gave up everything, and he never cared, never listened to me, or cared about the things I wanted, needed. Now he's gone, and he's still taking things from me. This house is all I had, I scrubbed and polished every inch of this place every single day, and neither of you even noticed. Fingernails all brittle and stained. All so it could actually look like it was worth a dime. So, people could come inside and not see the dirt we tracked in from breaking our backs to put food on your plate. It was a hard life, but living it with someone you didn't even love anymore made it miserable. I know my life wouldn't be what it is now if I had gone to school like I wanted, maybe I could've become a nurse and made it on my ow—"

"So, what was your reason later?" Niya interrupted. "I didn't stay a kid, haven't been one for a long time. What was your excuse for not going back to school?"

Anita dropped whatever piece of clothing she held and raised up from the bed. Niya swore she felt a wind whip against her skin as her mother rose, taking small steps towards her.

"No answer for that one, is there?" Niya stepped closer to Anita. "You see, it's easy to point the finger. I didn't take any opportunities away from you. Slowed them down, sure. But stop, no, and neither did Dad. You liked your life. Maybe you didn't get everything you wanted, but you got enough to gloat and rub it in the faces of any and every church sister you had. But maybe when I got older, people weren't talking about those hats and out-fits anymore, maybe they started talking about your daughter. Her schooling, new job, new book? Dad told me about the way it bothered you, the way you'd roll your eyes and say it was like you didn't exist anymore. I'm not going to sit here and let you martyr yourself on my behalf; you're jealous of your own daughter's success and her relationship with your husband."

"You watch your mouth," Anita said as her nostrils flared.

Niya only then realized how close the two of them were, practically nose to nose. She felt her mother's heated exhale polish her chin and stared right back at her. Their glares were strong and rigid, inches between their eyes and blinks a seemingly made-up action. Niya felt her heart racing and wondered if Anita's was as well. Her skin felt like it was burning, the friction of the room pressed too closely upon her.

"Or what?" Niya straightened her posture, accentu-ating the height difference between them. "I'm not that eight-year-old hiding from you under the blanket anymore."

"What are you then?" Anita responded. "What are you but an ungrateful girl that never cared about anything besides herself? A girl who never once asked her mother what her dreams were, didn't even ask her father? A girl who didn't tell her mother she was cutting her husband open, having some stranger reach inside him and pull what was left out, before she laid him to rest? He filled your head with so much self-righteousness, you can't even see past your own nose. You say I always wanted everything to be about me, the woman that clothed, fed, bathed, and worked like a dog for you. For those schools, those jobs, those books, and that movie. No, Aniya. If everything was about me, then my life would look a whole lot more like yours."

Niya felt her insides rattle. Everything was shaking except for the room, she thought. She looked down at her hand and saw that it was as still as her mother's. It was like an elbow to her ribs, a shake only Niya could feel and only her mother could give. She turned around and headed out of the house, the way she never did as a teenager. Niya got in her car and peeled off with nowhere to go. She couldn't believe she had let this happen again. The buildup that lashed out with each turn and crooked back road she found to plow through. There were only two people in the world who had the ability to pull Niya out of her character, that could make her feel combative and outside of herself: her parents. The difference being her father never did. Niya parked in a barren lot, pressing her forehead to the wheel as the conversation swirled around her thoughts. The truths her mother found necessary to uncover after her father was dead, after Niya couldn't talk to him about it. Question him, understand him, hear him. The truths her mother decided to disclose when they couldn't be anything more than love equating to guilt. It was so ugly, and even though Niya didn't want it to, it hurt.

Niya saw tears trickle onto the steering wheel; they slid down like rain. They fell like they didn't know which way to go, drifting left and right even though the car was still. Niya wanted to touch one, to have it run onto her finger so it wouldn't feel so alone, so it could feel some comfort in its slow descent, but she didn't. There was no point because she couldn't hold it forever, and it seemed crueler to Niya to give it a thing she knew she'd have to take away.

Niya's phone rang. It was Colleen, but she sent her to voicemail. She couldn't handle any other news that day. Her world felt like a cesspool of other people's decisions, but that day was weighted in distinct ways. It was a day made to make her feel small, smaller than the world already had. She looked at the time, five to three, and the time struck a nerve. Jerome's offer to meet for coffee came swirling back to her like she was still standing in his office looking at her shoes. She'd forgotten all about it and was surprised it crossed her mind again. Niya decided to go ahead and do the thing she had decided not to. Anything would be better than watching the steering wheel cry.

She arrived at the hospital in about twenty minutes. Niya scoured the patio of coffee drinkers, surprised at how crowded the bistro was. There were mostly nurses and doctors, many still in their scrubs. She did another once-over and figured she was too late, but felt a quiet relief at the thought.

"Aniya," she heard the familiar voice shout from the far side of the patio.

Jerome was wearing sunglasses and a soft lilac button-down; Niya barely recognized him. He waved her over as she danced through the taken seats and slid into the spot he had saved for her.

"I didn't think you were going to make it." Jerome smiled.

"Neither did I." Niya forced a grin as she settled in.

Jerome pulled off his glasses and couldn't help but keep his smile on. His excitement, outfit change, and recently applied cologne confirmed what Niya knew deep down. It was a date, but anything would have been better than what was happening at home.

"What are you having?" Jerome asked as he handed her a menu. "The quiche is great."

Niya scanned the menu. "I think I'll just have something to drink."

She ran her fingers across the assortment of teas but couldn't settle on one. Niya wanted something stronger, something to help wash away the taste of the day.

"Just a coffee for me," she said.

"How do you take it?"

"Black."

Jerome headed inside, and Niya was already checking the time. The more comfortable her chair became, the less her decision to go was making sense. Using Jerome as a distraction wasn't fair to him. Niya glanced at her car as she rested her chin against her knuckles and wondered if now was the time to escape—to disappear into the tiny town she imagined she'd have no real reason to return to.

"Here we go," Jerome said, returning faster than she expected.

So much for the escape. Niya shrugged to herself and lifted the coffee to her lips.

"How've you been?" Jerome asked.

Niya bobbed her head from side to side. "As good as can be expected. How about you?"

"Don't do that." Jerome took a sip of something that smelled light and sweet. "I didn't invite you here to talk about myself, Aniya. I'm here to listen if you need me to."

The comment surprised her. "I don't even know you."

He gestured in a *so what?* sort of way. "When my dad died, I was pissed off at everyone for no good reason either. It eventually transformed into actions and words that I couldn't take back. I think it would've done me some good to talk things through and to not be made to feel wrong for feeling how I was. Even if it wasn't warranted."

"I doubt that's true." Niya sipped her coffee. "I'm sure there was a reason for how you were feeling, Jerome."

"Maybe." He let out a little laugh. "What about you? What's your reason?"

Niya wasn't sure what it was, the patio laced in powdered blue scrubs, Jerome's unassumingly sweet smile, or the smell of her coffee tied into what might have been his latte. Something reminded her that sometimes it wasn't about vulnerability, it was just about talking.

"My mother." Niya squeezed the cup. "She always gets under my skin, but today was something else."

"What happened?" he asked, casually.

"She just unloaded a bunch of shit about my dad." Niya exhaled. "Him not being there during the pregnancy and when I was first born, just a lot of stuff."

Jerome nodded. "That must have been hard for her."

Niya's eyes shot up at Jerome's; it wasn't the kind of empathy she expected. "Yeah, but she only brought it up because he left the house to me."

Jerome sipped his drink. "That must've been hard too."

Niya squinted a bit, not sure what was going on. "I guess. But then she started blaming me for her life and lack of opportunities and anything else not going her way."

He nodded. "I see. That's what did it then, right?"

Niya nodded and shrugged at the same time.

Jerome put his cup down. "I doubt she really blames you for those things, she's grieving and probably feeling like she came in second place or something."

"Yeah, but that's insane."

Jerome nodded his head. "It's human. Doesn't mean it's right, but it just *is* sometimes."

Niya felt the coffee heating her up. "I get that, but there's just no reason that can excuse her behavior.

She always does this, picks fights, and throws horrible baggage I have to drag around just because. She's my mother, it's just not okay."

Jerome lifted his hands and tilted his head. "Hurt people hurt people."

The words almost tiptoed across the table. Niya stared at Jerome's mouth, remembering the motion it made when he said something Niya couldn't believe she was hearing for the first time. She was sure Jerome hadn't come up with the phrase himself, but that didn't make it any less soul churning. Why hadn't Niya seen it before? Whether it was grief or the long-standing issues Anita had carried since before she was born, her mother's hurt transcended the two of them. Niya wondered if her own did the same thing.

Jerome went on, "That's usually reason enough. Sounds like your mother had a rough go of it, and that stuff doesn't get resolved for most people, especially not us. It gets buried because we don't know what else to do with it, where else to put it, so it just keeps hurting."

Niya sat with Jerome's comment. Just sat. The words continued to ring and seemed to be on repeat, the duality of them, repetition of a trend. Being so much like the other and so different. Niya put her nose to the coffee and let the smell fill her up the way it had the night before. She inhaled, and for the first time wondered why Anita didn't empty Jacob's coffee mug, clear his favorite records, or tidy his sweat stained clothes. She wondered why the shed remained untouched and why Anita herself didn't volunteer to read the eulogy. The words rang like a chorus, harmonizing so sweetly inside of Niya she thought she had swallowed honey.

"Hurt people hurt people," Niya said. "I've never heard that before."

"You'll never guess who said it to me." Jerome grinned again.

Niya let out a sudden laugh before she pulled it back in. Nothing was funny, but it came out anyway. She hadn't laughed in days, so in some way, it was nice to know it was still a reactionary response. Jerome's grin turned into a smile again, and he almost got a full one out of Niya. They both sat quietly then, drinking their sweet and bitter respites, reminiscing about the fathers that no longer were.

The two chatted for the rest of the afternoon. Niya took Jerome's card but was doubtful she'd use it, though she had been doubtful about meeting him at the coffee shop as well. When she got home, Anita wasn't there. The house was still, but the windows were open, and the breeze brought the curtains to life. They rippled and even lifted high enough for Niya to stand beneath them. She only watched, but the motion still comforted her. She peeked into the kitchen before heading for the stairwell. The sink was empty. Niya took hold of the banister and clutched it tightly. She dragged her hand all the way to the top, the subtle imperfections not so subtle anymore. Niya stopped in front of the guest room and eased the door open.

To her disbelief, the room was empty. Every box disappeared like it had never existed. What was left were the sheets and old blanket resting on the foot of the bed. Still unmade and untidied. Niya sat down and spread her arms across the sheets, slowly rubbing them and picking up the satisfying friction they left behind. She reached for the blanket then, it was stiff and woolly, and opened it up. She turned her body and eased her feet beneath it. She wanted to recoil at the discomfort, but she pushed her feet down further. Her legs followed, and soon, she was pulling the rest on top of her. Niya laid back as the old blanket covered her, and she felt the impulse to close her eyes. So, she did. She closed her eyes and covered her face and didn't wonder why. Niya laid beneath the blanket, and though it was difficult from time to time, under the wool's thick and heavy texture, she breathed. She just laid there and breathed.

Part 7

Anita

The words pushed out of Anita like they belonged to the world and had no place being inside her, not anymore. She listened to her daughter storm out of the house and wondered if it might have been the wrong time to unload everything. Jacob was her hero. The pillar of hard work and resilience that Aniya had built much of her own work ethic by, but he was also human, flawed, which was a reality Anita believed her daughter needed to be reminded of.

Anita looked around the newly decorated bedroom and admired her handiwork. Since Jacob had moved into the guest bedroom, Anita was finally able to follow through on the vision she had for their home, or at least a small portion of it.

She started collecting new pieces for the room with the savings she'd put aside after working part-time at a few department stores. Most of the furniture she found was oak, deep and slightly varied shades of the wood that balanced well with the room and the rich reds and gold lace accenting the light from the front facing window. Anita found the bed and dresser at a thrift shop, the bed was disassembled and maneuvered into a corner of the store with the dresser keeping it from sliding onto the floor. The pieces were blanketed in thick layers of dust, and Anita left countless smudged prints throughout the inspection of the furniture. Although seemingly untouched for years, likely forgotten in the back corner, Anita knew quality when she saw it. She called Jacob and got him to bring the truck, the bed and dresser were going with her.

After finagling the pieces into the bedroom, Anita had changed into her house clothes and began to scrub through the dresser's grime. Her bucket of warm, soapy water quickly transformed into a murky puddle of residue Anita could no longer see her reflection in. Her hands were soaked, and her cuticles mirrored the oak's shade as the wood came to life in Anita's otherwise lifeless room. She cleaned the unassembled bed pieces next, wiping down the crevasses and corners of the oak until they were spotless. Anita had to dump and fill the bucket in the hallway bathroom a dozen times before she was done, but her new furniture was cleaner than she imagined it had been in decades. Anita had found some old wood polish and slowly began painting the dresser with thin layers, gently buffing a quality of furniture she'd never owned before. Her movements were slow and meticulous, the repetitive circles she made did not leave a single area of the wood surface dull. The dresser was exquisite, a hidden gem covered in cobwebs and debris from its environment, but a pure and unseen treasure amidst the rubble. When she was done, Anita stared at the finished dresser and smiled to herself before pushing it into a new corner in which it would not be forgotten.

Anita wasn't able to buy pieces as grand as the dresser when Aniya was young. She'd find little antiques and smaller items, but she'd always get an earful whenever it was something as extravagant as a table or chair. The process would usually start with Jacob eyeing the item, not saying whether he liked it or not, but rather inquiring about where she bought it and how much it cost. He'd eventually go on about how their money needed to be spent on important things, not things that were important to her. Things like clothes for Aniya, food for the house, the essentials. Anita never understood how treating herself to something special from time to time always equated to a lecture, especially from a man that constantly bought and restored old cars.

"It's not the same, Nita," he'd say as he drove some beat-up old jalopy into the driveway.

Jacob would work on car after car, selling them just as fast as he got them. That was his reasoning, anyway. He would make money off of the cars, but they both knew that wasn't all it was. He found joy in restoring, looking for compatible parts and bringing a vehicle back to its former glory. Jacob found as much happiness in restoring old cars as she did in finding antiques. It wasn't about the money, it was about him, and Anita wished she could have kept something that was just about and just for her.

She had put the bed together next—not the easiest feat considering the lack of instruction. Jacob had loose nails and tools all around the house, so Anita managed to find what would fit and hold the new bed together. She'd already found the perfect duvet and used her employee discount to acquire the duvet that would top the new bed. It had taken her the entire weekend to put together, but when she finished, she knew the early stages of her room remodel was exactly what she had needed—something that was hers.

Anita opened the new duvet after building the bed and spread it out before lifting the corners and watching it float down. She lifted it again, throwing it towards the ceiling, and thought of Aniya, the way she would rush into the room whenever she was making the bed. She'd jump and crease the perfect lining that Anita had made, leaving shallow little footprints all over the freshly cleaned and pressed sheets. Anita remembered running her off most of the time, not knowing when she'd have time to wash the sheets again with her schedule at the mill. She remembered a day she let her play under them though, in the guest room under a set of sky-blue sheets Anita knew no one would dirty too fast. Anita watched her duvet fall that day and thought of calling her daughter, checking in about her latest book or whatever she was working on, but she decided against it. She was sure Aniya would call her father soon, and Jacob would give her all of the updates.

This was the first time Aniya had seen her room since she'd spent years finding all of the pieces and turning it into a space she always wished she had. It was the first time Aniya had seen something that was totally her own, and they had fought in it, the space she had built, the space Anita doubted her daughter would be in again. Jacob was gone, and there was no reason for her to come back, especially now. It had always been that way. Since Aniya could walk, she had followed behind her father like he was the only parent she had. Anita used to think that besides sharing a few letters in their names, the two had nothing in common, even when Aniya was a baby. She was just like her father, from her laugh to her smile and features, and something about that rubbed Anita the wrong way.

Jacob's initial distancing regarding Anita's pregnancy was the first time she'd experienced that side of him, a cold brashness he never evoked in all their time together. He almost seemed like a different person. Whenever she imagined Jacob in the early days it was always in his car. He'd pick her up in that huge old Buick and the two would just drive. Anita would feel the wind rush against them as Jacob leaned away from the wheel, grinning from ear to ear as the two headed towards the horizon. They'd drive for hours sometimes, filling up wherever they could find a gas station as long as it was away from an old sundown town they knew to avoid. They'd laugh and talk for hours about nothing but the speed of the car and the way it felt to be moving towards something.

It was when Jacob said, "You're always going in one of these, and life is so full of not going—it's sorta magical to be in control of a machine that's sole reason for being is to go and to help you go. I love cars, Nita. I've never felt so free," that Anita understood just how much she loved him, how much she understood him, and how much they had in common.

It wasn't until Jacob found out about the pregnancy that the other side showed, a side he would become all too familiar with showing Anita, especially near the end of his life. It wasn't that he was mean all the time, it was that he'd forgotten that he loved to go, to move and experience the world around him. Anita began to resent that. After Aniya began living her life, that was enough for Jacob, to hear the stories of the places she traveled and what she wrote during her residencies. In reading her essays about the waters out east and mountains to the north, Jacob felt he'd done all of the same things she had. He'd talk about the way she wrote about the places she loved in such detail and with such care, he could smell the ocean right from his porch.

"Who needs to go anywhere when they can live everywhere?" Jacob said once while reading a piece of fiction Aniya had written. "She gives us the whole world, Nita."

"No," Anita replied. "She gives you the whole world."

Jacob couldn't understand though, the time and experiences that Anita felt they had lost out on. The adventures that should have been theirs too. The distance between the old Jacob leaning back in the *Deuce and Quarter* and her then husband eventually became the distance that settled between them. The difference being, Jacob had Aniya, and Anita had nothing. So, she took to the house, scraping up for vintage wonders from around the world that they could share. Little pieces of adventures and histories living with them that could transport Anita to all of the places she never got to see.

Aniya had been gone for more than twenty minutes, and Anita was sure she wouldn't be back for quite some time. Aniya had gotten into the habit of taking off after a disagreement when she was in high school, usually with her but sometimes with her father. Jacob would fumble around the dark outside until he found her and patched up whatever hole Aniya told him Anita made in her; holes Anita didn't believe existed. Maybe it was just a different time, a different generation, but Anita could never wrap her head around the fact that a child as loved as Aniya was, could ever feel truly hurt by a parent. A parent that loved her. Anita figured it was just another means for Aniya to get her father's attention—she had it her entire life, why should it diminish as she got older? If Anita was constantly poking holes in her, it meant Jacob would constantly be filling them back up, and the line between what caused a hole became fainter and fainter. At first it was the way Aniya said Anita spoke to her, then it was the things she asked her to do, and eventually it was the way she looked at her.

"Stop looking at me like that, Mom," Aniya once said.

"Like what?"

"Like you can't stand me."

"I'm just looking at you," Anita replied. "Would it be easier if I just pretended you weren't here?"

Aniya took off, and there it was, another hole the day before her seventeenth birthday. Anita stopped knowing how to do anything right with Aniya almost as soon as she could walk, and the past few days after Jacob's death had been no different.

Anita walked out of her room and made her way down the hall. The guest room door was cracked, and she glanced inside at the mounds of boxes filled with the remnants of her husband. Anita pushed the door and immediately smelt him, his stale coffee breath and too robust cologne. Had her eyes been closed, she'd swear she was pressed against his chest. The boxes were stacked throughout the room and there was a bag with a few mementos edging the corner of the bed. It looked as though Aniya had put it to the side for herself. Anita stepped away from the door and thought about going inside, just for a moment; to surround herself with all that was left of him, to grab a few pieces of the last days of his life, but she couldn't. She couldn't ever since the morning she called him down for breakfast, and he never came. When she growled from the bottom of the stairs before knocking at his room door with fury she didn't need to be in. She hadn't gone back in that room since she walked in and knew he was gone. The way his body slumped so still it couldn't have been asleep. The man she'd known for almost forty years, the only one she'd loved and despised and cared for and wished ill on, the only one that had given her *la petite mort* and told her its name in French because he knew she'd find the English version too crass. The man she shared a daughter, life, and home with, the one she used to drive into the sunset with, was gone. She hadn't been back in there since that day, and Anita wasn't sure if she'd ever go back in again.

She made her way downstairs and turned on the kettle. Anita preferred her tea with honey, heavy spoonfuls that would run over before they made it to the mug.

She sipped it slowly and let the steam rise up into her nostrils, helping her to breathe through the lingering smell of Jacob she could still taste. Aniya had asked her what to do with the boxes before she took off, and Anita still wasn't sure. She thought about having the neighbors come by and pick through the belongings, but it was too similar to vultures swooping in and cleaning up a corpse. Plus, Anita didn't need or want all of those people up in the house. The house.

She thought of everything again and became as hot as the tea. Anita didn't want Aniya to think that she had a problem with her father leaving her the house, but she couldn't help but feel as though Jacob had taken something else from her. All Anita had was the property, the home they shared their entire lives. Jacob had Aniya, a bond and love he had threatened to never give his daughter, but he had her anyway. Anita knew that about him, and he knew that about Anita. For Jacob to give away what he knew was hers was a sort of low that pushed Anita's grief into the realms of rage. Mostly because there was nothing she could do about it. Anita looked out the window while sipping her tea and tried to think of what Jacob might have done if she had been the one that died. A way she could have taken away the thing he knew he'd have, Aniya. She sipped again and thought that all she could do was write a letter, a letter telling Aniya the truth about how her father was when he found out she was coming. Anita paused and lowered her mug. A letter spelling out everything she had told her daughter that very day.

Anita closed her eyes and placed the mug on the counter. She rubbed her bare face and instinctually checked her palms for lipstick and powder residue. Anita had already done the worst thing she could have to Jacob, and to Aniya. So much of their conversation was a blur to her at that point; Anita wasn't even sure how it had escalated so fast. She didn't regret it though, telling her a truth she should've known years before; she only regretted the how and the when. Trickling off the back of her father's death wasn't the time, and she knew her daughter would never forgive her for it. Anita picked the mug back up and drank the rest of the tea until she reached the bottom. She took big mouthfuls of warm honey and felt it drip down heavily inside of her.

Her cell phone rang, and Anita dug the device out from her purse on the kitchen table.

"Hello," she answered.

"Hey, you," a familiar voice replied. "How you been?"

"I'm alright, Richard, how about yourself?"

She could hear him grin through the phone. "I'd be better if you finally started calling me Sleet."

"Neva'," Anita said back.

Anita hadn't seen him since he emceed the service. They'd grown closer in the later years of Jacob's life, which is why he was adamant about Anita calling him by his nickname, Sleet. He got the nickname as a teenager when his uncle told him he wasn't as smooth as he thought he was, he told him he was more on the slippery side, like sleet. He loved the name and went by it from then on. Not with Anita though, who immediately asked him what his real name was when he first came by to play spades with Jacob and a few other work friends. Anita didn't care if he didn't like it, she wasn't about to be calling a grown man the same thing people called a type of snow. Their friendship remained casual and consistent through the years, with Sleet sometimes taking Anita to church when Jacob was working on the car, and she needed a ride. Sleet thought the world of Jacob. Anita could tell. They were nothing alike, but he was like a big brother to him, the two only being a year or so apart. Sleet's playfulness and extroverted personality seemed coy next to Jacob's often domineering way, but they were great friends, the type that would undoubtedly leave a space when one was gone.

"Richard, I have a favor to ask," Anita said.

"Anything."

"Can you come by and clear out the boxes from Jacob's room?"

"Are you sure?" Sleet spoke kind of low. "You don't wanna keep 'em?"

Anita replied, "No, I just want them gone. Donate them, throw them away; I just want them out of here."

Sleet paused. "No problem. I'll be there in a few minutes."

Anita hung up and twisted the long handle of her purse around her wrist before making her way up to her room and sitting at her vanity. She'd never owned one until she began remodeling when Jacob moved out of the room, a decision that had caught Anita off guard. She had just returned from church to find Jacob moving piles of his belongings into the guestroom.

"What are you doin'?"

Jacob grunted as he laid an armful of clothes on the bed. "Just movin' my things in here; it's too cramped in the bedroom."

Anita asked, "What do you mean too cramped?"

"All my records and all your makeup stuff," Jacob replied. "It's just too much, we need a bit of space. Don't you think?"

Anita didn't remember how she responded, just that she was the only one sleeping in their bedroom from then until Jacob's death some eight months later. So, she slowly began filling the room with things she otherwise wouldn't, including the vanity. Anita's love of makeup and the ability to sharpen her already smooth and defined features was one of the many things she enjoyed about wearing it, but she mostly liked change. The various shades of red lips and smokey eyes that could match her mood or mask an emotion, there was power in choosing how to present oneself. A power neither Jacob nor Aniya understood. Anita opened her foundation and began lightly applying a layer to her skin—she didn't need much. Then, she grabbed her red velvet shade and painted the edges of her lips before filling in the rest. Anita glanced down at the lipstick tube and then back at herself.

"That's a pretty color on you," Jacob said a week before his death.

Anita paused, a bit caught off guard, "I thought you didn't like when I wore lipstick."

"I never said that," he replied. "Just never saw the point. But that color, it suits you, Nita."

Anita remembered watching him go back to reading his paper and sipping some too strong coffee as she left for the grocery store. The way he didn't even notice that that was the first time he'd made her smile in months. Anita felt her eyes become foggy as the memory faded, and she only saw herself in the mirror. She looked at herself and wished she had said thank you to him that day, for seeing her, for in his own way, telling her he still thought she was beautiful. Anita held the tears fighting to get out and wished she had thanked him for so much more. She heard a knock on the door and headed down to let Sleet in, passing the room filled with all that was left of her husband one last time. Anita glanced inside his room a final time and knew she'd lost more than just Jacob, more than his favorite records and coffee cups. Anita was losing the biggest piece of her daughter she had left, a piece that manifested in Jacob, the one tie the two seemed to have to each other. It wouldn't just be the room that was left empty when Sleet was done. Anita was sure of it, as sure as she was that red velvet was the only shade of red she'd ever wear again.

Part 8

Curtains

"Are you sure this is what you want to do?" Wilbur asked.

"I am," Niya replied, gripping her cellphone.

"He wanted you to have it, Aniya."

She exhaled. "And I do, but I want her name on the deed too."

Wilbur hesitated before he said, "Alright. I'll get the paperwork sent over. Have a safe flight."

"Thank you, Wilbur," Niya said before she hung up.

Niya stared out the car window. She always thought graveyards looked smaller when empty, even though people said the opposite. They covered a good deal of land, but in the scope of corpses seeded into the planet, they were such small spaces. Scenic hillsides, blips of the living, and tiny reminders of our inevitability. Niya picked up the newspaper next to her and figured she'd go ahead and get it over with.

The cemetery was barren, as Niya assumed it would be at that time of the morning. Anita was still asleep, well, was still in her room when Niya left. It didn't occur to her to go knock or let Anita know she was flying out after she made a stop. They hadn't spoken since the explosion, and Niya didn't see the point in shallowly forced goodbyes. She called Wilbur on her way to the cemetery. It was a small thing to have Anita's name on the deed; that would go a long way.

Niya walked through the graveyard as she skimmed the paper for the obituary section. She had been in contact with one of the editors prior to the funeral and had gotten the okay to have her father's eulogy printed in place of a standard obituary. A part of Niya wondered if the leniency was due to her name, if someone had recognized it or had a copy of her book on their desk. It was a shame that a kind act couldn't just be a kind act, but Niya had noticed more of them after she topped the bestseller list. It irked her sometimes, the preferential treatment and its clash with her ethics. Not that time, though. When it came to the eulogy, she quieted her conscience and ignored the ethics. She knew it was hypocritical, but figured she would stomach the hypocrisy if it meant her father could be acknowledged the way she knew he'd prefer.

Niya approached the grave and tried her best not to think about the last time she was there. The tears of other people often proved one of the biggest triggers for her own, even the thought of their tears could be enough. Niya had a purpose there, and to continue in external grief wasn't a part of it. She didn't believe in talking to graves or the optimistic drivel that acted to help someone release what they had pent up. She didn't go there to ask him about all the things her mother told her, if their marriage was really an ultimatum to be in his daughter's life, if her mother getting an education threatened him that much, if a little of what Anita said was true, if some of his love was just guilt manifesting itself in the most beautiful way. Niya didn't go there for that. She owed something to her father. She knew he would've wanted her to write his eulogy, and she let him down by not sharing it when she had a chance. So, she owed it to him to read it aloud, at least once. Niya folded the paper back and swallowed a mouthful of nothing before she began to read:

Anyone that knew my father, Jacob Lewis, knew he was not a man of few words. Much of his life was made up of anecdotes and old stories, and then retellings of the times he told those stories and anecdotes. Years ago, when we had an off the cuff conversation about eulogies, he told me what he didn't and did want in one. He didn't want it to be a biographical list: place of birth, birthdate, and all the other things that people who already knew him would know. He didn't want to be known as the final living child of Henry and Edna Lewis, that his brother, Carl, died in a car accident and his sister, Jessie, of breast cancer. He didn't want to be remembered as a career, traveler, or volunteer. He wanted to be remembered for two things: his love of cars and his love of family.

The first time my father drove a car on his own, he was nine years old. His father would make deliveries for local farmers, and he would get my father to help. One day, my grandfather was not feeling well and handed my father the keys to his pickup. He didn't say much of anything, knowing my father already knew the routine. So, he got in the truck, pulled the seat up as far as it could go, and revved up the engine. He told me it was the first time he understood how powerful he was. That the buzzing of the truck ricocheted through his hands and into the rest of him. Then he took off, flew down the dirt path faster than he had any business going, and for a second, he told me he knew how it felt to be free. Really free, and it was unlike anything he'd experienced in his life, and ever would.

His love of family was a much quieter one, definitely no revving, but a powerful experience. Where the car offered him his first freed experience, it was with my mother, Anita Lewis, that he said he first felt peace. He wasn't sure if it was the sound of her voice, the way she moved to Soultrain albums, or the way her hand felt in his. Whatever it was, he told me he thought he knew what it meant to be at peace, until he met her, until he loved her. As for me, his only child, he said it was simple, really. That he could die tomorrow, and he'd be okay with it, because he knew I was okay. He said that he could die without regret, because he knew that he got the only thing that mattered right.

He wanted to be remembered by these things, not because they were his favorites or they mattered most, but because they taught him that life could only be what we choose to make it. There's so much injustice, hate, inequality, and every other crippling reality we face, but when you feel the freedom in grounded and wheeled flight, holding the hand of the person you love, or sharing a coffee with your kid that's not a kid anymore, you get to live. You get to live, and you get to choose for it to be enough. More than enough. For a few moments, you can choose to be happy. My dad didn't know what life would be if we didn't choose that when we could.

Niya pulled the paper towards her chest before looking down at his grave again. She hadn't thought about it until then, but it was Niya's only piece of writing that her father hadn't read. She folded the paper and squeezed it between some of the already wilting flowers, holding onto the little time they had left. Niya closed her eyes and held in all of the broken pieces she knew were coming undone. Her rattled ribs and burning eyes and shaking lips and bubbling blood and unsteady heartbeat. She looked at the ground he was deep beneath and wanted to say goodbye, to call him by his name one more time. To feel it leave her body like it wasn't something she'd never be able to say again. *Bye, Dad.* It rang through her and bounced off of those broken things, shattering them to mere remnants of themselves. Niya pursed her mouth and refused to let the words come out. She refused because she couldn't stand knowing the way it would feel if she let them free.

Niya turned around and walked to the car, faster than she intended. When she reached for her phone to start up the directions to the airport, she saw two missed calls from Colleen. Before Niya got a chance to call back, she heard the phone ring as she pulled out of the lot.

"Hey, Colleen," she answered, eyeing her phone for directions.

"Hi," Colleen replied, her excitement uncontainable. "I have news!"

"What's up?"

"They're keeping the title," Colleen almost sang.

Niya smiled. "I'm glad to hear it."

"But..." Colleen's excitement dipped. "About the mother..."

"Well?" Niya just wanted to hear her say it.

Colleen sighed as she said, "They're writing her out. I'm sorry."

Niya pulled out into the main road. "It's not your fault. What did they say?"

"She wasn't vital enough to Tulie's story."

"Ouch!" Niya jokingly exclaimed. "I get it. Seems like she should have been, though."

Colleen tentatively spoke, "I know, they all agreed tha—"

Colleen's voice faded as Niya pulled up to a red light and a brightly decorated storefront caught her eye. It looked like an upholstery shop, lavishly tinted and patterned furniture occupying the window. Niya's eyes were drawn to the bold shades as they popped on the otherwise dull street before the highway. She glanced at a pinstriped sofa set with soft gold trim, accent pillows, and a well shined dark wood desk with a matching purple seated chair. Before she turned her attention back to the road, Niya spotted them. Draped over the side of an armchair in the far corner of the arrangement, delicately adorned red curtains. Niya was too far to see the details clearly, but the red was deep and rich, like an ocean that forgot it was supposed to be blue. They painted the display so starkly, Niya couldn't believe she didn't notice them right away. Then an inkling touched her, just for a second, to pull up and venture inside the shop, but it left as quickly as it came.

"Aniya?" Colleen raised her voice a bit. "You there?"

"Sorry, Colleen. I got distracted." Niya pulled off slowly, just realizing the light was green.

"Is everything okay?" Colleen asked.

"Yeah." Niya flipped her signal light on and turned off on the highway. "I just saw some curtains that I think someone might like."

"You should grab them," Colleen said. "You have

some time before the flight."

Niya pursed her lips again before she exhaled and replied, "Not today, but maybe another time."

Colleen went on about production, and Niya took the next exit onto the highway. She pressed her foot to the gas and felt the vehicle kick forward in a way that exhilarated her. Niya smiled a bit as the wind from the crack in her window kissed her cheekbones and ran across her skin. She would have closed her eyes and relished in what she felt had she not been behind the wheel. Niya sped up and felt the wind brush against her like it wasn't a stranger; it touched her like it wanted to leave its fingerprints behind, like it wanted her to know it was there.

Acknowledgements

I would like to thank the Stillhouse Press team for all of their work in preparing this book for publication. Of that team, I would like to acknowledge Brenna Fuhr, for championing this narrative, Linda Hall, for her support throughout, and Eunice Kim, for her keen and careful eye and kind and understanding ear. Special acknowledgements are also paid to Paul and Dennis, as our novellas occupy the same box set and words remain intertwined in this process. Deepest thanks to my mother, Lorrie, for reading and rereading the manuscript, as she usually does. Lastly, I would like to thank Sivale McEwen for her insights and perspectives as the story came to life.

About the Author

Morgan Christie's work has appeared in *Callaloo, Room, The Hawai'i Review, Sports Literate*, as well as other publications. She is the author of four poetry chapbooks and her first full-length short story manuscript, *These Bodies* (Tolsun Books 2020), was nominated for the Hurston/Wright Legacy Award in fiction. She is the 2022 Arc Poetry Poem of the Year Prize recipient and her poetry chapbook, *when they come* (Black Sunflowers Press 2021) was featured in the Forward Arts Foundation's National Poetry Day exhibit. Her collection *People Without Wings* is the winner of the 2022 Digging Chapbook Series Prize and her essay collection *Boolean Logic* was the 2023 Howling Bird Book Prize Winner (November, 2023).

9 781945 233265